The Curse of the Scarlet Scarab

By Angel Favazza

The Curse of the Scarlet Scarab
By Angel Favazza

All rights reserved. No part of this book may be reproduced or transmitted in any form or by any means, electronic or mechanical, including photocopying or recording or by any information storage and retrieval systems, without expressed written consent of the author and/or artists.

The Curse of the Scarlet Scarab is a work of fiction. Names, characters, places, and incidents are products of the author's imagination. Any resemblance to actual events or persons, living or dead, is entirely coincidental.

Story copyright owned by Angel Favazza
Cover illustration by Brian Quinn
Cover design by Marcia A. Borell

First Printing, March 2025

Hiraeth Publishing
P.O. Box 1248
Tularosa, NM 88352
e-mail: hiraethsubs@yahoo.com

Visit www.hiraethsffh.com for online science fiction, fantasy, horror, scifaiku, and more. Stop by our online bookstore for novels, magazines, anthologies, and collections. **Support the small, independent press...and your First Amendment rights.**

To my students, whose enthusiasm for learning makes every day an adventure and whose passion for knowledge fuels my journey as a teacher and writer. Thank you for asking about this book—it's a gift from me to you, reminding me why teaching is the greatest privilege.

1

The air crackled with magical energy, a combination of ancient mysticism and foreboding visions. In the depths of sleep, Ruby grasped the elusive scarlet scarab, feeling its rhythmic pulse resonate through her veins. This dream was unlike the others—a surreal yet hauntingly familiar experience, where the boundaries of reality blurred with the enigmatic secrets buried within.

A sudden jolt ripped Ruby from this ethereal realm. Her heart was racing, breath caught deep in her throat. The disturbing dreams that had haunted her for weeks left their lingering echoes. Each vision drew her closer to those ancient sands, beneath the moonlit embrace of the Nile, and always, always—the pulsating red scarab.

With a heavy sigh, Ruby sat up in bed, rubbing her temples, attempting to dispel the tendrils of the persistent dream. Casting off the heavy quilt, she swung her legs over the side of the bed and made her way toward the bathroom.

In the soft glow of dim light, she pivoted away from the bathroom mirror, reaching for her silver-filigree hand mirror. The delicate design faintly shimmered as morning light filtered through lace curtains, casting a subtle radiance.

Gazing into the reflective surface, her eyes focused on the small, red scarab tattoo gracing the nape of her neck. It had appeared the morning after her seventeenth birthday, coinciding with her first dream of the desert. The permanent crimson hue seemed to carry a mysterious message, a symbol of a story yet to be revealed.

As her finger absently traced the embossed patterns on the mirror's back, a soft clicking sound drew her attention. Captain Corvus, her pet raven, perched on the edge of the clawfoot bathtub. Its gears whirred softly as it cocked its head, observing her with its opaque black eyes. Ebony feathers so black it picked up a hint of midnight blue, reflecting the feeble sunlight, and a subtle ticking emanated from within its intricate frame. It flapped its wings, sending a gust of cool air swirling through the small space.

"Good morning, old friend," she greeted him with a weary smile, acknowledging the loyal companion who had seen her through countless adventures. Corvus responded with a series of clicks and whistles as if recounting tales of its own nocturnal escapades. She placed the mirror back on the sink, casting a fond glance at Corvus before continuing with her morning routine.

In the kitchen, Mollie was squinting with one eye open at the *London Daily Post* through a large magnifying glass.

The headline "Murders Again Double Event in London's East End" caught Ruby's attention and words like "Jack the Ripper" along with "Vigilance Committee." Ruby drew up beside her and let out a sigh. "The Ripper is at it again, is he?" she asked, glancing at the date, Sunday, September 30th, 1888, in the center of the newspaper.

"Right. But here... look at this," Mollie quickly flipped through the paper, stopping at a dog-eared page she had flagged. Bold letters announced the upcoming grand opening of Lavoie's Jewelry Emporium. "See," she continued, "this bloke, a Frenchman, is opening a high-end shop with 'rare' and 'luxurious' gems and jewelry."

"Sounds promising," Ruby chimed in, against the hiss of the steam-powered tea infuser. "Let's check it out." Her curiosity stretched beyond the mere baubles. As a seasoned jewelry thief, she found herself intrigued by the security measures a foreigner from France might employ. An enticing challenge—something she could not resist.

It had been nine years since the Tay Bridge disaster that had claimed Ruby's entire family, except for Mollie, her only living familial relation. Ever since the two cousins-in-law shared a portion of a brick warehouse in London's East End for £4 a week. The humble space became a testament to their close-knit bond, where echoes of laughter and whispered secrets created a sanctuary amid the harsh realities of their world.

Despite its unorthodox nature, their home held a peculiar charm and provided adequate comfort. Inside it was cleverly partitioned, providing ample space for their needs: a pair of expansive bedchambers and separate workshops tailored to suit each of their crafts.

In the seclusion of Ruby's room, she adorned herself in attire befitting their stealthy endeavors. She wore a crisp white blouse with billowy sleeves, their edges lined with golden threads. It was paired with a russet-colored waistcoat adorned with a meticulous arrangement of tiny, pulsating crystals along the seams, catching the light in a kaleidoscopic dance of color. Her beige skirt, paneled with durable fabric interlaced with conductive gray fibers, held a subtle shimmer as it flowed around her.

Her fingers brushed gently against the radiant emerald earrings, their intricate mechanisms resonating with a faint hum—a gentle nod to both refinement and her profession. With a last tug on her boots, she called out to Mollie, "Ready?"

As Ruby's fingers wrapped around the polished brass lever nestled within the wall, a faint click echoed, setting into motion a series of hidden gears. With a smooth, almost imperceptible buzz, the hydraulic bed began its graceful descent. Effortlessly, it folded into itself, seamlessly merging with the wall, transforming her bedchamber into a spacious and unencumbered space.

At that moment, Mollie emerged from her room. Her attire—a lemon-yellow satin dress with white lace neckline and cuffs. The garment hugged her frame, accentuating the cinched waist and the subtle puffs that adorned the sleeves. The voluminous hemline boasted a delicate yet robust hoop skirt mechanism, allowing the fabric to hover just above the ground as she moved, showcasing her polished gray-button boots.

A pair of pearl earrings shimmered in the light, exuding an effervescent glow that lent a touch of timeless elegance. Her small poke bonnet featured mirrored cogs and a wide white ribbon neatly tied under her chin complemented her upturned nose, golden curls, and cerulean eyes. Mollie adjusted her bonnet, a smirk playing on her lips. "You seem surprised."

Ruby chuckled, a playful glint in her eye. "It's a rare occurrence when I'm not the one waiting on you."

Mollie's grin widened. "Oh, don't get used to it. I'll be back to making fashionably late entrances in no time."

Ruby raised an eyebrow teasingly. "I'd expect nothing less. After all, punctuality isn't your strong suit—unlike that bonnet, which suits you perfectly."

"Why, thank you, Ruby Red!" Mollie replied, offering a complimentary curtsey.

It was hazy that Saturday morning, the temperature warm, humid really, but not uncomfortably so. The remnants of early morning rain veiled the bustling streets of London in a low-lying fog. The city moved like spectral silhouettes in the dull daylight, with steam-driven conveyances emerging from the mist accompanied by a mechanical clip-clop clatter. The damp cobblestones glistened, echoing the footsteps of passersby and the distant blows of whistles in the urban haze.

As their horseless carriage smoothly glided to a stop, they found themselves in the fashionable West End of London, precisely on Regent Street. The jewelry store, as depicted in the black and white drawing from the paper, stood before them. After paying the driver two shillings, they gracefully exited the carriage and stepped out into the bustling street. The ornate sign hung above the entrance, its letters gleaming in gold against the dark, polished wood of the storefront.

Through the window, they saw the glittering grandeur of a crystal chandelier casting its radiance over rows of glass cases displaying a dazzling array of jewelry. Balloon chairs, draped in rich tapestries, dotted the space, and tall jade vases overflowed with apricot-colored trumpet lilies.

Mollie marveled at the opulence within,
"Looks like a dream in there."

"Let's hope their security is more substantial than their French decor," Ruby muttered smugly, adjusting the waistcoat over her blouse.

"I thought we weren't targeting this one," Mollie said, raising an eyebrow.

"We're not," she replied, squinting through the glass. "This is a brand-new *French* boutique, so it's a prime opportunity to evaluate their security." She adjusted her hairpin, a sleek contraption concealing an array of miniature tools within its frame.

Entering the jewelry store felt like stepping into another realm. Their parasols, crafted from silk and equipped with a blade in the handle, found their place in the mechanized drying stand, emitting a discontented whir as they settled in.

Ruby's attention was drawn to the central display case, showcasing an impressive assortment of brooches embellished with opals, lapis, turquoise, and intricate designs—abstract dragons, elongated birds sporting jade and pearl eyes, all gilded with a mix of silver and gold foil.

The tranquil ambiance of the store was suddenly disrupted by a deep, melodic voice resonating from a tuxedoed automaton. "Miss, may I help you?"

"Yes, please. May I see that one... the star," Ruby gestured towards something truly exquisite, a star-shaped brooch, its brilliance catching the light like a hundred stars.

With a push of its cuff link, the automaton unlocked the case and placed the eight-point star sapphire and diamond-encrusted brooch in its palm. It spun slowly shimmering like a piece of the night sky. Just as the question about the star brooch's cost lingered in her mind, her attention was abruptly seized by a luminous red scarab amulet.

It was as though the universe had pivoted its focus from one celestial marvel—the starry brooch—to another. The red scarab amulet glimmered with an ethereal radiance, its crimson hue infused with a curious glow that captured Ruby's gaze, drawing her into its mesmerizing aura.

The amulet was a masterpiece of meticulous craftsmanship. The beetle, carved from a precious gemstone, perhaps a pigeon's blood ruby, appeared to pulsate with its own vitality, emitting an iridescent shimmer beneath the store's ambient light. Its fiery red hue seemed to glow from within, like a living ruby.

2

As Ruby admired the exquisite beauty of the scarlet scarab amulet, Mollie deftly surveyed the store's security measures with practiced discretion.

For them, these defenses were mere hurdles, obstacles waiting to be overcome. Ruby's expertise in bypassing locks and security systems had evolved into second nature, honed by countless daring exploits.

They understood that stealing jewelry was a complicated dance that went far beyond the mere thrill of a heist. It entailed a choreography of precise steps extending beyond the initial snatch and grab.

After all, the pilfered pieces weren't satisfied with a swift getaway. They demanded artistry, a metamorphosis, a rebirth within the underground world of the shadow market. With finesse and artistry, Mollie turned purloined treasures into unrecognizable masterpieces, a transformation that could deceive even the keenest of observers.

Leaving Lavoie's, the bustling street enveloped them in its vibrant energy. The sun, having dissipated the morning fog, bestowed a cheerful golden glow upon the rows of polished windows. Mollie went on regaling Ruby with descriptions of Lavoie's bracelets and rings with a vibrant energy, but Ruby's thoughts bent on one thing—the mesmerizing scarlet scarab amulet.

As their conversation unfolded, they found themselves strolling the narrow corridors of Piccadilly Circus. Ruby stopped suddenly and looked out across the street at the row of elegant shopfronts flaunting elaborate displays. "Mollie, I've changed my mind," she interjected. "We're robbing Lavoie's."

"What? You can't be serious," Mollie said. "I thought we were just scouting it?"

"That scarab amulet—it's changed everything. It's a sign, tied to my tattoo and my dreams. And more importantly," Ruby paused again, gathering her resolve, "it's a challenge I can't ignore." She searched Mollie's face for any sign of empathy and found it. "Besides isn't that what keeps us going? The thrill of the unknown?" She smiled, hoping to sway Mollie, as her pulse raced with excitement.

Mollie interjected, her grip firm on Ruby's elbow, her voice earnest, "Lavoie's security systems are no joke. We only saw a fraction of what's there. Those walls—" she paused thoughtfully, "the walls there's something inside of them, something that we've not tackled before."

"I understand the risk, but that's exactly why we must," Ruby asserted with conviction. "Taking this chance, it's worth it. The amulet—it's as if fate is guiding me, and I can't turn away from its call," she declared.

Mollie countered. "I don't know, it's a huge risk," she said, "I'm worried. You know how unforgiving the prison-house is, especially for girls like us."

"This is it. Our big break. A chance to finally carve our names at the top."

"Top tier, eh? Fancy that," she acknowledged, the excitement beginning to twinkle in her eyes.

Seizing the advantage, Ruby pressed further. "Picture it. Enough treasure there to set us up in a respectable place, a proper home." Then she painted a vivid picture, one that contrasted with their warehouse abode.

That settled it.

"Tonight, we raid Lavoie's."

By late afternoon, downtown buzzed with its usual vibrancy. Ruby and Mollie navigated the labyrinth of streets, finding their way home amidst swirling chimney fumes and towering brick buildings.

That evening in the early hours of the evening, the girls prepared, geared up, and ventured back downtown. In the city, dusk was but a fleeting interlude. The sky turned from pale plum to gunmetal gray in a matter of minutes, the dark descended like a black velvet curtain.

Nightfall brought a different crowd to the streets—a rougher, more hostile presence. Navigating London's nocturnal maze, women seldom ventured, yet Ruby and

Mollie were exceptions—always vigilant, always armed. Ruby's fingers traced the contours of her pistol, a reassuring presence against the hidden threats of darkness.

As they approached Lavoie's, the city's heartbeat softened to a hushed lull, leaving only the distant echo of hoofbeats and the gentle purr of distant carriages.

The timing was perfect.

Ruby whispered forcefully but hushed, "Now."

Mollie retrieved two small vials from her boot—one filled with a crystalline powder and the other carrying a silvery liquid. With a mischievous glint in her eyes, she expertly blended the contents and applied the compound to the steam-powered padlock.

Ruby's general rule of thumb was to avoid steam locks. Their scalding emissions could last for minutes, making them rather hazardous. Thanks to Mollie's compound, though, the lock fizzled and popped open within seconds. She gave it a gentle nudge with her toe and with a subtle hiss the door swished open.

Ruby pulled Corvus from her reticule, setting it down, and with a subtle twist of a hidden gear, it awoke to survey the area with its multi-lens eyes, scanning for any signs of alarm or movement. Once Corvus gave the all-clear chirp, they proceeded cautiously inside.

As they navigated the dark corners of the store, their steps quiet and calculated, Ruby withdrew a compact lantern from her reticule. She adjusted the lens of the lantern, fine-tuning its focused beam. With a soft whistle, the lantern came to life, emitting a beam of light that carved their path through the darkness, its silent, crystalline mechanism allowing them to remain concealed in the shadows.

Corvus perched atop Ruby's shoulder, occasionally tilting its head, or extending a metallic wing, changing her course with a soft shake as it surveyed their surroundings.

Mollie wielded a pneumatic-powered crowbar, as she deftly pried open hidden drawers seated beneath display cases. With a whisper of escaping steam, the tool amplified her strength, revealing concealed compartments with a series of soft mechanical snaps. Quickly she sprang into action, activating her high-speed bagging apparatus. Gems and jewelry were drawn in with voracious hunger, swallowed into the device's depths.

Corvus nudged Ruby gently with its beak, its eyes equipped with imperceptible shifting lenses capable of scanning for hidden mechanisms and obscure surveillance devices. A soft series of clicks reverberated as it relayed information, a subtle language only Ruby understood.

With a sudden flutter, Corvus hopped down, deftly pressing its beak against a concealed wall panel. It slid open revealing an office veiled in intriguing shadows. The dim glow from Ruby's lantern played across the room, painting the secrets with a rich indigo hue.

Hidden rooms held secrets longing to be unveiled, and this one was no exception. It was well-organized and elegantly furnished. She scanned the bookcases, the desk at one end, and stacks of newspapers and empty boxes. Yet, her unwavering focus was on finding the safe. The silent chant, "Safe, safe, safe," echoing in her mind intensifying the thrill of the hunt.

She slowed, as with each step, the gears whirred in the walls, a testament to the building's ingenuity, while cogs hummed with concealed energy, driving the mechanisms of the hidden office.

There!

Nestled within a dark recess, edges meddling in with the darkness, stood a cast-iron safe, its sturdy design beckoning with a promise of concealed riches.

The bolt lock, though deceptively simple in appearance, bore the hallmark of fine craftsmanship. Its gears and levers held whispered secrets, an enigma that only a seasoned locksmith might decipher. A tingling anticipation rushed through her: the thrill of the theft mingling with the looming suspense of discovery.

3

Ruby knelt in front of the safe and got to work. She spread a leather tool roll out on the ground beside her and surveyed the lock. With a pair of tension wrenches and a spring-loaded pick, she delicately probed the mechanisms of the safe. Each twist and turn was met with subtle tension and then a dance of gears, the dim light barely illuminating the complex workings within.

Flipping a switch on her goggles, the lenses glowed softly, enhancing her vision. Applying just the right pressure, she maneuvered the picks with precision, aligning the cogs and levers to their intended configuration. The safe responded with faint clicks and subtle shifts, a symphony of mechanical movements, until finally, the heavy tumblers fell into place within the mechanism with a satisfying clunk, granting access to the secrets concealed within.

With a tug, the heavy door groaned open, revealing emerald rings, diamond bracelets, and the star-shaped brooch that had caught her eye earlier. Each piece was swiftly and deftly stowed away inside a covert panel in her skirt. But
the one-piece she sought above all others—the scarlet scarab amulet was nowhere to be seen.

Suddenly a voice pierced the air, uttering a single word that was all around, *"Blood!"* Startled, she whipped around, pushed her goggles onto her forehead, and glanced around the room, but there was no one in sight—nothing but eerie silence.

Despite the unsettling sensation of being watched lingering in the air, a sense of urgency propelled her to refocus once again on the safe. That's when she noticed something peculiar inside—a box lay open, its presence inexplicable, seemingly materializing out of thin air.

When Ruby got close enough to reach for the box, the voice started up again and then fell silent. The inside of the box was dark. It looked empty. She pulled her goggles back on and squinted her eyes, leaning forward to get a better look. There. Something glinted in the far corner of the box.

It was the scarlet scarab amulet!

As Ruby reached inside, a sudden surge of energy flowed through her frame, jolting her senses. In that brief, disorienting moment, a startling vision consumed her thoughts—she saw her infamous great-great-grandfather, Thomas Blood, the audacious thief of the Crown Jewels. He sat at the base of an hourglass, sand relentlessly cascading over him, marking the passage of time with an inescapable rhythm.

An abrupt, high-pitched squawk from Corvus shattered the surreal experience, its frantic wing flapping echoing through the room. The amulet remained nestled within the box, its enigmatic presence adding to her daze, leaving her struggling to find her bearings once more.

Seeking stability, Ruby leaned against the wall, drawing in a deep breath, but panic surged through her as she glanced toward where Mollie was positioned. A shadowy figure approached menacingly behind her.

The automaton!

Its presence now towering ominously large. Reacting instinctively, she slammed the safe door shut, the metallic clang reverberating through the room, and sprinted towards her.

"What? What's going on?" Mollie asked, completely oblivious to the looming automaton.

"Behind you!" Ruby's words burst out as a frantic yell.

Mollie twisted aside just as the automaton's limbs surged forward, swiping the air where she had been a moment before. The automaton's movements were a blur of polished brass and whistling steam.

Suddenly, muffled clanks and electric buzzes resounded down the hallway and throughout the store as smoke bombs erupted from hidden compartments, shrouding them in heavy opaque smoke. "Smoke bombs!" Mollie cried.

"Here!" Ruby tossed her a gasmask infused with alchemical breathing oils and secured one on herself.

Mollie hastily donned the mask as the smoke surged, engulfing the entire store. Through her mask, Ruby watched Mollie give a fast look at the safe, a moment of hesitation in her eyes.

Ruby shook her head impatiently. "No! Run!"

As they ran toward the door, thick clouds enveloped them. Corvus soared down from a concealed alcove, its wedge-shaped wings whirring with precision cutting a path for them to follow. Amidst the chaos, they relinquished the mysterious scarab amulet and the tuxedoed automaton to their fates, swallowed by a whirl of enigmatic turmoil and technological havoc.

As they stumbled back home, the feeble light of dawn trickled through the windows of their East End warehouse. Dropping her toolbelt and waistcoat on the floor, Ruby felt the burden of the night's chaos bearing down on her shoulders. Meanwhile, Mollie, worn out from their heist, sunk silently into an armchair, the exhaustion radiating from her in palpable waves.

Despite the coolness of the room and the weariness clinging to every limb, the soft glow of the gas lamps lent the room an inviting warmth. With a rumble in her stomach, Ruby set about preparing breakfast, the sizzle of bacon soon joining the familiar aroma of freshly brewed Darjeeling tea.

Mollie's fatigued smile mirrored Ruby's sense of relief, the comfort of food and companionship easing the tension that still lingered. She sighed, her gaze fixed on the cracked ceiling, and said, "Well, that was a disaster waiting to happen."

Ruby nodded, sinking onto a nearby wooden crate. "You can say that again. I can't believe we nearly got ourselves killed. What the hell were we thinking?"

Mollie shot her a wry smile. "In our defense, it seemed bloody brilliant at the time."

"At the time," she said, shaking her head.

"We've had worse," Mollie quipped, attempting to lighten the mood. "Besides we nicked enough jewels to put us in a good way for a while."

Ruby sighed. "True."

Mollie's pretty face turned serious. "Do you still feel like everything—that scarab amulet, the dreams, the tattoo—are somehow connected?"

Standing at the sink, Ruby paused and closed her eyes. Her thoughts swirled around the notion of returning, of securing that scarlet scarab amulet. But convincing Mollie to accompany her presented an entirely different hurdle.

"Well?" Mollie's gaze urged for an answer.

After a moment's hesitation, Ruby replied, "I think so. I know so, yes." She drew in a decisive breath. "I have to go back."

Mollie grabbed a slice of bacon and snapped off a bite. She chewed thoughtfully and then swallowed. "But, Ruby, going back there means exposing ourselves to more danger. Lavoie and his lot won't take kindly to another intrusion. We barely made it out last time, and their security's a wild card we can't predict. Are you sure you want to be part of this?" Her eyes pleaded with Ruby, expressing the depth of her concern for her cousin's safety.

Ruby grappled with her decision, which hung delicately in the balance. Though she harbored a fierce determination to find answers, even if it meant facing the unknown alone, caution prevailed in Mollie's presence. "No, I suppose not," she replied, choosing to hold back the full extent of her intentions from Mollie for the moment. The scarab amulet's mysterious charm called to her, but she realized the need to tread carefully and gather more information before exposing Mollie to the potential dangers that awaited them at Lavoie's.

Mollie took a sip of her tea. "Alright then," she said with a relieved smile.

Soon after, alone in her room, the cool, crisp, white illumination of electric lights highlighted a wobbly stack of leather-bound tomes chronicling aeronautical achievements. Occasionally, Corvus graced the scene, perched atop the volumes like a guardian sentinel. Her bed stood adorned in chartreuse and taupe striped linens, surrounded by the remnants of her craft—leather scraps, naked wires, and an array of mismatched rivets and cogs.

Ruby loosened the laces of her well-worn leather boots, their weight feeling heavier than usual against her tired feet and tossed them in a corner. She unraveled the disorganized tool roll. Amidst the assortment of miniature tools, tinted lenses, and range of lockpicks, she carefully arranged each item within the roll. Each tool found its designated spot secured beneath tiny cogwheels, each gear serving to hold the items firmly in place. It ensured they remained organized and ready for use at a moment's notice. With practiced ease, she secured the roll, tied it, and set it aside.

Sitting in bed, Ruby carefully inspected her recent acquisitions, scrutinizing each piece of jewelry through a loupe hanging on a long silver chain. She examined the sapphire forget-me-nots woven into filigree rings, slender gold and diamond bracelets, and a pair of brooches. Ten exquisite items lay before her, each a testament to fine craftsmanship and luxury.

Gazing reminiscently at the portrait hanging on the wall, the daguerreotype's mirror-like surface reflected her family. Nestled inside a frame crafted from pieces of driftwood she had gathered along the beach over a decade ago. A warm rush of happiness flooded her as she recalled frolicking in the foamy waves with her parents and her baby sister—a cherished memory frozen in time. It remained the last and only photograph she possessed of them.

The clock ticked.

Breaking away from her memories, she discreetly secured the stolen jewelry within a hidden compartment nestled within her Venetian desk clock.

Ruby sank into her bed, she closed her eyes, but the details of the heist replayed incessantly in her mind, like a recurring melody from a music box. The image of the abandoned scarab amulet lingered hauntingly, teasing her thoughts, and eliciting an overwhelming sense of regret for having left it behind. Its enigmatic power and the potential connection to her red scarab tattoo and persistent dreams refused to fade away.

As slumber pulled her into its embrace, Ruby drifted into the realms of dreams, finding herself, once again, in the desert. A gentle breeze brushed against her skin, carrying the whispers of a majestic palace adorned by soft moonlit shadows. Amidst this surreal scene stood a hooded figure, clutching a silver coffer adorned with glowing white hieroglyphs. The figure suddenly vanished in swirling billows of ash and dust, leaving the gleaming box nestled in Ruby's palms. Strangely, while still dreaming, she became filled with an inexplicable longing to vanish into the unknown, much like the hooded figure.

As she awoke, a sudden hot sensation on her neck drew her attention—a faint, persistent ache emanated from her tattoo. She cautiously traced the lines of the design, its permanence on her skin begging for answers, whispering secrets of an uncharted destiny.

4

By the light of day, London felt fresh and full of promise. Ruby and Mollie traversed through East London's foremost bazaar, Petticoat Lane Market. They sought a welcome diversion from the previous night's blunder.

Mechanical stalls adorned the main thoroughfare, showcasing a variety of gadgets and captivating trinkets. Ornate horseless carriages rumbled along trailing billows of vapor that mingled with the heavenly aromas of roasted nuts and sizzling meats. Among the crowd, eyes caught glimmers of gold and silver pocket watches and flashing jewelry. While these pieces were aesthetically pleasing, they failed to meet the standards Ruby and Mollie were accustomed to.

Amidst the gentle hum of machinery, the aroma of freshly brewed tea beckoned them toward a charming tea and crumpet cart. Glistening gears adorned the cart, ticking in harmony with the soft clinks of porcelain teacups. As they savored the sweetness of the cakes, their attention turned to an approaching marvel—an automaton ballet troupe, their graceful movements orchestrated by the gentle hiss of steam released after every plié and pirouette.

Mollie's eyes sparkled at the sight of a menagerie of mechanical circus animals. Nudging Ruby gently with her arm. "Aren't they absolutely precious?"

Ruby nodded. Her gaze shifted between a bear with sad glass eyes wearing a tutu, walking on its front paws, and a set of precision lock picks.

As they wandered along, Mollie was drawn to punch-pliers and corkscrew augers, while Ruby found herself engrossed in a display of ornate skeleton keys, each one a masterpiece catching the sunlight and casting baroque shadows. She singled out a few. But then her attention was captivated by one in particular—the bit of the key was surprisingly razor-thin, and its ebony bow featured a tiny red gem. "How much for this one?" she asked, pointing.

"Oh, that's a beauty, lassie," the merchant replied in a heavy Scottish brogue. "It'd be two shillings." A bargain indeed. Ruby paid him, clipped the key to a dangling copper chain of her chatelaine, and continued with her stroll.

"Ooh, what's that?" Mollie's attention was suddenly captivated, enticing her away like a bee drawn to a rosebud. The sounds of children laughing and oohing and ahhing surrounded her as she delighted in the battle between a sword-laden prince and a steam-breathing dragon. Melodies from a street musician's calliope tubes filled the air, adding to the lively atmosphere of the surroundings.

Even in this seemingly serene setting, Ruby's senses stayed vigilant, attuned to any subtle signs of potential pickpockets. The bustling crowds were a haven for those adept at their craft—masters of disguise, blending seamlessly into the throngs. Their tactics, though often simple, were executed with precision. A sly bump, a swift grab, exploiting moments of distraction, like a parent chasing after an energetic child or revelers in high spirits, provided them with ample opportunities.

"Ladies! Yes, you!" A boisterous vendor called. His exuberant expression was framed by a thick, unkempt beard peppered with specks of gray. Bright, animated eyes glinted with enthusiasm as Ruby and Mollie walked toward him. As they came closer, Ruby's eyes widened in surprise and delight. He had an assortment of ancient artifacts.

Egyptian.

"Step closer, lovely ladies, and feast your eyes upon these wonders from the land of Thebes—or rather, Egypt," he chimed in, his stout figure brimming with energy despite the beads of sweat glistening on his forehead in the mild chill of the midday air.

Mollie, intrigued, picked up a peculiar statue—a man's figure with the head of a falcon. "Who's this then?"

"Ah, that is none other than the revered god Horus, guardian of the pharaohs," he exclaimed with an air of solemnity. "Handle with respect, my dear. These gods demand our reverence, above all else."

Pointing to a striking deep turquoise statue portraying what seemed like a mummy with crossed arms and finely painted details, Ruby inquired, "And this one?"

"A keen eye indeed! That, my friends, is an Ushabti —a sacred statue often entombed with the deceased to serve in the afterlife," he explained.

Ruby's focus shifted momentarily when, like a phantom from her dream, an ominous hooded figure passed within her periphery. But, in an instant, the shadowy form disappeared, a mere fleeting glimpse—a dark silhouette against the vibrancy of the market. Yet, when she turned to mention it to Mollie, there was nothing but the usual array of patrons and stalls. Mollie hadn't seen a thing, her attention entirely ensnared by the artifacts on display.

"These statuses," the vendor enthused, his eyes bright with passion, "each holds a story, a saga of ages past. They've witnessed the rise and fall of empires, held secrets buried for millennia, and beheld the mysteries of forgotten worlds."

Mollie held one of the statues close to her ear, jesting, "I wonder what tales they'd tell if they could talk."

"Indeed," Ruby laughed, admiring a statue of a catlike goddess. "And what about scarabs? Any in your collection?"

"The scarabs," the vendor mused, his voice carrying a hint of reverence. He raised his hand, fingers delicately weaving through the air. "The intricate markings, the designs—they conceal untold narratives, etched into the sands of time, waiting to be uncovered and understood," he remarked thoughtfully. "Sadly, none today, but come back, and I shall have a table full of scarabs waiting for you," he said cheerfully.

As they left the marketplace, a persistent feeling of being watched pricked at Ruby's skin. The mysterious figure in the hooded cloak triggered an uncanny recollection, resembling the figure from her dreams. Was he following her? Who could he be? And more pressing, what was his intent?

The sunrise painted a delicate golden hue across the horizon, marking the end of another restless night for Ruby. The image and power of the scarab amulet were ever-present in her thoughts. She needed answers—she needed to go back to Lavoie's. The pull of the amulet's mysterious charm was too strong to resist, despite the potential dangers that lurked within.

Knowing that Mollie wouldn't approve of her risky decision, Ruby resolved to venture alone. The desire for answers eclipsed her apprehensions, and with each step toward Lavoie's establishment, the mysterious allure of the scarab amulet intensified.

5

And so, embracing the arrival of dawn, Ruby quietly slipped out of the warehouse. Her auburn curls, neatly fashioned into a low, loose chignon, strategically veiling the cryptic tattoo. A doeskin cropped suede jacket the color of weak tea, set off the pale green embroidered leaves of her beige high-neck dress, creating a calculated contrast with the richness of her hair.

By the time Ruby reached Regent Street, the city was fully awake. Moving through the throng, adeptly weaving among the clusters of people, Ruby approached Lavoie's Jewelry Emporium, the passersby parting to make way for her resolute stride. Suddenly, a distinguished gentleman intercepted her arrival, stepping right into her path with an air of calculated determination. His sophisticated attire caught her attention—an ocher-colored coat tailored with copper-lined lapels and an ivory shirt adorned with red gemstones that glittered in the early morning light.

"Mademoiselle Blood, might I have a word? I am Monsieur Lavoie," he announced in a French accent resonating with an air of urgency amidst the street's clatter.

Surprised by the familiarity with which he addressed her, Ruby refused to allow herself to warm under the pressure. "Yes, Monsieur Lavoie, what is it?"

"Last night's escapade," he began, his voice lowered to a hushed tone. "Your entry into my establishment, a daring feat indeed."

Her body stiffened, an underlying sense of unease creeping into her stomach. "I assure you, sir, I am not one for idle threats."

He smiled mockingly. "Ah, but there's no need for threats, Mademoiselle. Merely an exchange of services," he said, his words like a well-rehearsed symphony.

"What sort of services?" she asked, masking her apprehension.

"I believe a misunderstanding has occurred," he stated with a calculated pause. "One that could benefit from our mutual cooperation."

She arched an eyebrow. "Cooperation?"

His lips curved into a knowing smile. "Your skills are unparalleled, Mademoiselle. But they could serve a greater purpose."

She kept her composure and asked calmly, "And if I refuse?"

He leaned slightly in, his voice a mere whisper. "Then the authorities might find you and your friend's expertise, let's say, rather incriminating, especially when dealing with a certain rouge amulet." His hand guided Ruby in the direction of the shop. "Let's have a few moments in private before people start gossiping," he said, winking at her and making her feel uneasy.

Her heart raced. The weight of his words was heavier than the jewels she stole last night. "What is it that you want?"

"Assist me, and any past missteps will be forgiven," he declared. The doors parted at his approach as if they yielded to his unspoken command.

Stepping into Lavoie's shop, a sudden sting pricked from Ruby's tattoo, a curious warning that hinted at unforeseen consequences. As he guided her down the hallway, Lavoie was halted by a concealed panel. With a subtle wave, the panel slid open, revealing the hidden office.

"Assist you?" she asked.

Motioning for her to enter, she hesitated briefly before stepping forward. "Mademoiselle, please, have a seat." He gestured towards a leather chair behind the polished mahogany desk and settled into one himself. "Your reputation precedes you. Your adventures have turned into whispered tales. I require your expertise for a venture of grand proportions."

Although reluctantly flattered, she remained cautious, "And what venture might that be Monsieur?"

He leaned forward, so close that Ruby could see a thin scar edged through black stubble from his temple to the curve of his dimpled chin. "The acquisition of an artifact that could change our destinies."

Her curiosity piqued, Ruby inquired, "What sort of artifact?"

"One from an ancient Egyptian tomb, one believed to hold immeasurable power," he said, running his hand through his black windswept hair. "But retrieving it will require someone of your unique skills."

She twisted in the narrow seat and looked over her shoulder, weighing his words. "You speak in riddles, Monsieur."

He smiled knowingly. "Consider this an invitation to unravel those riddles, to unearth secrets lost to the sands of time."

"But why me?"

"Because, Mademoiselle Blood, you possess a gift for the extraordinary, as evidenced by your connection to the scarab amulet. Your lineage, your exploits—each detail paints a portrait of someone destined for remarkable adventures."

Ruby ran her finger around the stiff beige collar that banded her neck and fidgeted her shoulders beneath the soft napped jacket, feeling the weight of his words. "You certainly do know a lot about me."

"Only what is needed to recognize potential," he remarked, his reserve cool, eyes hard as flint.

"And what do you expect in return?" she asked.

A slow grin curving his thin lips. "Your expertise in acquisition, an adventure that will unravel history's secrets. But rest assured, my resources shall be at your full disposal," he assured, pulling from his pocket a folded piece of parchment, no larger than a pound note. He opened it and smoothed the surface and edges flat on the desk.

A map of Egypt.

Ruby's eyes fixed upon its cryptic markings hinting at untold adventures. His proposition swayed between allure and ambiguity. The scarlet scarab etched on her skin seemed to resonate, echoing the pulse of the unknown.

Lavoie leaned in, his eyes flashing with a mix of eagerness and cunning. "I need someone with your unique talents to assist me in this enterprise, one that will most certainly benefit us both."

Every instinct warned Ruby of the risky path ahead, but an undeniable curiosity tugged at the edges of her resolve. He awaited her response, his gaze fixed on hers with a mixture of anticipation and calculated charm. She held his gaze for a moment longer than what was comfortable, wrestling with conflicting emotions.

"I must confess, Monsieur Lavoie, your words raise more questions than answers," she replied, cautiously keeping her guard up. She looked down, smoothed her skirt, and then looked at him. "What *exactly* do you expect from me?"

He eased back into his seat, a subtle shift in his demeanor from eagerness to composed sophistication, a transition that whispered of his seasoned shrewdness. "Ah, Mademoiselle, as I've mentioned before, your gifts are truly unparalleled. I seek your extraordinary talents to retrieve a certain ancient Egyptian artifact, an object of unparalleled importance."

"You want me to travel to Egypt for some trinket. Why can't you just send for it?" she inquired.

"Ah, it is a delicate matter, and the challenge for you will be uncovering its hidden location," he explained.

"What artifact?" she asked, her cheeks flushing as her frustration mounted. "And how on earth am I supposed to find it in the blooming desert?"

He tapped on the top of the map and pointed, "See these X's? They mark two potential locations." He leaned back slightly, and continued, "Mademoiselle, you must recover the scepter of Pharaoh Aketankhen Neferet."

Against every instinct, she couldn't help but feel a pang of intrigue, like a moth drawn to a mesmerizing although deadly flame. "Go on," she whispered.

Lavoie continued, his voice carrying a tinge of urgency. "This artifact, hidden somewhere in Egypt, holds secrets that could shake the very foundations of power. I require someone of your adeptness, your skill in navigating shadows and uncovering hidden treasures, to retrieve the pharaoh's scepter and return it to me." His gaze lingered on her, scrutinizing everything from her face to her boots, and her stomach turned.

While she couldn't deny the allure of his words, the eclipse of doubt lingered, a nagging reminder of the potential dangers lurking within such an undertaking. "What's in it for me?" She pressed, seeking clarity amidst the layers of ambiguity.

Lavoie's lips curved into a wry smile, revealing a glimmer of satisfaction at the inquiry. "Ah, Mademoiselle, I offer more than just mere compensation. You and your comrade shall keep the stolen jewels, and I shan't involve the authorities. But understand, this artifact bears profound historical and let's say lucrative value—it's not merely an item. It's a key, metaphorically speaking, naturally." His gaze, probing yet calculating, searched for her response.

"Forgive me, Monsieur Lavoie," she began cautiously. "The prospect you present is undeniably intriguing, but the risks loom large. You've revealed some aspects of this plan yet left the crux of your request veiled in ambiguity." His demeanor remained composed, a mask concealing the depth of his intentions. "Yet, Monsieur," she said, "the risks inherent in such an undertaking cannot be disregarded. What guarantees do I have?"

Lavoie's crooked smile bore a hint of a cunning gambler. "Ah, mon chéri, in this world of shadows and secrets, guarantees are as elusive as the artifacts we seek. But trust me when I say your efforts shall not go unrewarded. Consider this an opportunity to reshape history's narrative." Evil shimmered off him in waves, but more than evil. Danger. Polite, yes. But he had already proven there was far more to this proposition than Ruby had expected.

6

"Monsieur Lavoie, I ask for time to consider your proposition," she responded, her tone laced with an air of guarded determination. "The risks you speak of demand a thorough investigation and serious consideration."

With a subtle nod, he acquiesced. "As you wish, Mademoiselle. Take your time. But remember, opportunities such as this seldom knock twice."

With a murmured acknowledgment, Ruby took her leave, the weight of Lavoie's proposition echoing in her mind like a tether linking a falconer with his bird of prey—beckoning her toward an unexpected and perilous quest. Despite the undeniable dangers that lay ahead, the venture brimmed with untold possibilities, casting an enticing allure that she couldn't easily ignore.

The similarities rolled through Ruby's mind, prompting a sobering realization. She couldn't deny the similarities between herself and Lavoie. Both possessed a clandestine nature—cunning, streetwise individuals who knew how to navigate the precarious world of high stakes, unafraid to manipulate chances or unapologetically bend the rules. As the thought settled, an age-old adage echoed in her mind: "There is no honor among thieves."

But n

ow, she faced the daunting task of conveying the absurdity of Lavoie's mission, the not-so-subtle threats of blackmail, and the hazards of international travel to her cousin. Convincing Mollie to partake in this reckless endeavor felt like an overwhelming feat, an uphill battle against reason and common sense. The gravity of the situation pressed on Ruby's shoulders, and she spent the evening gathering her thoughts before broaching the delicate subject with Mollie.

The next morning, the two girls nestled into the velvety plush, high-backed chairs of London's premier tearoom, The Aerated Bread Company. The space was a fusion of old-world opulence and modern innovation, where the polished wood and brass fixtures gleamed under the soft glow of Edison bulbs encased in glass electroliers.

Tea orders were deftly dispatched through the pneumatic tubes snaking along the ceiling, a marvel of pneumatic engineering. With a gentle whoosh, the tubes carried capsules of tea blends, each labeled with precision and dispatched to their respective tables. The teas themselves were steeped into a concoction producing flavorful steams, promising a unique sensory experience with every sip.

As they waited, the mechanical hum of the tea-dispensing machines accompanied the lively tick-tock of an oversized pendulum clock that adorned the back wall. The air was infused with the comforting aroma of a myriad of teas, wafting from brass-hinged caddies displayed on ornate wooden shelves.

With a satisfying clink, their teacups were ceremoniously placed on their table, the steam rising from the brews swirling in delicate thin wisps as the
heavenly aroma of mint and citrus enveloped their senses.

"Okay, out with it. What's the story?" Mollie's voice dripped with concern as she delicately sipped her Ceylon leaf tea.

Stirring her tea with a dainty silver spoon, the aroma of bergamot calmed Ruby's nerves. "I had a chat with Lavoie. I know I know..." she sighed. "He's aware of our heist and he's dangling a proposition over my head. If I say no, we're both taking the fast track to Newgate."

"Prison?" Mollie's voice dropped to a whisper. She pondered a moment. "We got enough enemies without the law on us, too."

"Exactly. Plus, there's an Egyptian scepter in the mix. Valuable. He wants us to pinch it for him."

"Who's got it?" Mollie asked, taking another sip of tea.

"He wants us to hop over to Egypt," she said.

"Egypt? Just like that?" She chuckled, nearly choking on her tea. "Oh, splendid!"

"Yep, off to Egypt we go," Ruby replied, her hand absentmindedly cradling the tattoo on her neck. "Maybe I'll crack the scarab mystery and find out how it ties into me. Or stumble upon something that'll make sense of all this."

"Don't be a blooming idiot! He'll sell us out the minute he gets what he wants," Mollie voiced her concerns, a frown etching deeper lines on her forehead. "There's nothing to stop him from double-crossing us."

Ruby sighed again, exhaling the tension. "I know. It's a risk for us both. If we mess up or get caught, he loses his precious artifact, and we go to prison. But if we succeed, it's a mutual victory. He gets what he wants, we walk away unscathed, and claim our reward."

"Reward?" she asked, arching a brow.

"Yes, we keep the stolen jewelry. And you know, that's worth a small fortune."

Mollie glanced at Ruby, her eyes filled with uncertainty. "I don't like being blackmailed. Besides Lavoie's requiring us to do something downright dangerous."

Ruby struggled to articulate the extent of her desire, her need, to accept the offer. Feeling the pressure grow heavier with each passing moment, her mind reeled.

Mollie's gaze softened. "Ruby, you're smarter than that. You do have a choice."

Ruby hesitated, took another sip of tea, and then spoke, "I need to learn all about this pharaoh and understand what we're really getting into before accepting this deal."

"Where can you find information like that?"

"I guess at the library," she replied. Mollie's eyes met hers, a silent reassurance passing between them, affirming their unspoken pact to face whatever challenges lay ahead, together.

As they left the café, the clinks of their teacups setting into a receptacle resonated softly. The streets, once alive with mechanical marvels and steam-powered conveyances, now appeared quieter, and more subdued, mirroring Ruby's mood. She exhaled slowly, though she didn't completely relax. Regardless of Mollie's feelings for Lavoie and his plan, Ruby knew that fate had woven an intricate tapestry, and she was but a mere thread being pulled into a destiny that awaited her.

The next morning, Aldermanbury Street was cloaked under a dense blanket of fog. The misty shroud wound itself around corners, meandering lazily down the damp cobblestones. Horse-drawn carriages moved at a sluggish pace, their progress hindered by the limited visibility, struggling to discern even a few feet ahead.

Amidst the misty, atmospheric backdrop, Ruby ascended the steps of Guildhall Library, anticipation fueling her steps. Upon entry, her eyes eagerly scanned the shelves, searching for volumes that might hold the keys to unlock the ancient mysteries she sought.

A strange sound momentarily drew her attention to a small figure on a nearby table—it was remarkable, a clockwork cat that appeared to be napping while its gears purred softly. "Looks like someone's enjoying a siesta," she remarked with a grin, nudging the cat gently with her hand exposing its name tag, *Herodotus*. In response, the cat lazily opened one eye and then shut it. "Seems Herodotus takes relaxation as seriously as research," she chuckled to herself.

At that precise instant, the library was stirred by the echoing caw of a bird reverberating through the aisles. And there, emerging through the shelves, was Captain Corvus, its ebony feathers casting a dark shadow as it descended, landing gracefully atop a precarious stack of waiting books.

"Corvus, what mischief are you up to?" Ruby asked, her voice full of amusement, as she observed it hop onto the table where the slumbering cat lay, waddling its way toward Herodotus. As Corvus approached, Herodotus gave an indifferent flick of its tail and continued its pseudo-sleep. Ruby shooed Corvus away and turned her attention back to her search.

Lost in the quest for ancient Egyptian lore, Ruby hardly noticed the approach of a young man, his arms laden with volumes.

"Miss, can I help you find something?" His voice, gentle and curious, cut through the silence of the library, a striking contrast to the hefty volumes he balanced.

Ruby turned to meet his gaze—a gaze that was hard to pull away from, the gentle sconce lighting accentuated the warmth in his hazel eyes. He appeared slender, dressed in a midnight blue waistcoat adorned with copper stitches and brown striped trousers. His hair was a rich sable, and nearly wild with curls, framing a face that appeared not much older than hers.

7

"Yes. I'm looking for books on ancient Egyptian," she explained.

A smile formed on the young man's lips as he nodded, leading her with a gesture toward a section crowded with leather-bound tomes, each promising to reveal history's mysteries. "Here you are, a wealth of information," he said, his tone carrying an eagerness to assist.

Ruby nodded, her gaze skimming over the titles etched in gilt, their dimpled leather spines adorned with cryptic hieroglyphics. "This is perfect. Thank you." Her fingers traced the embossed titles as if seeking a hidden connection to the past within their gilded markings.

He observed her enthusiasm with quiet interest, a faint smile playing on his lips. "Fascinating subjects, ancient artifacts," he remarked, setting down the stack of books on a table.

"Yes, indeed," she agreed, grateful for the company in this scholarly sanctuary. "I'm Ruby, Ruby Blood."

"Asher Salt, assistant librarian extraordinaire," he introduced himself with a congenial handshake, a shared spark of curiosity dancing in his eyes. "What are you working on? Research for college?" His assumption about her scholarly pursuits made her chuckle inwardly—she hardly looked like a college student pursuing a certificate.

"Something like that," she replied vaguely, not quite prepared to reveal the complexities of her search for information on the enigmatic pharaoh. "It's more of a passion project, really."

He nodded and a knowing warmth passed between them. "I understand a passion for history. It's a treasure hunt all its own."

Near the archive section of the library, they reached a corner where Asher laid out the gathered books on a table. Ruby saw that the cat now nestled itself on a chair at their table beside a stack of chronicles. Asher's gaze followed hers, a fondness in his eyes as he noticed her curiosity. "Herodotus here is my companion in unraveling these marvelous tales," he said, patting its head.

Ruby gestured upwards. "Ah, Captain Corvus shares a similar interest in my adventures," she remarked, a knowing smile gracing her lips. Corvus observed Herodotus with cautious intrigue from atop an adjacent bookcase.

"Seems our feline friend isn't interested in avian companionship today," she mused, smirking as she observed the distance between them.

Asher muffled a laugh in his hand. "Ah, the eternal standoff between cat and bird," he said, causing her to turn and meet his gaze that roamed over her face, a shared amusement shining in both their eyes.

They sat shoulder-to-shoulder, perusing the selected volumes, shutting out the world. Ruby observed Asher with a gentle grin as he brushed his hair off his face while scanning the pages. His brow furrowed at the slow pace with which the electric page-turner's arms were working.

When it came to men, like a firefly drawn to the darkness, Ruby was captivated by brooding, Machiavellian spirits—members of street gangs, opium eaters, and bare-knuckle boxers.

She relished the freedom from the burden of pretending to conform to what her late parents would have deemed 'good'—a facade she no longer endured. There was a certain allure in a man who understood the art of pushing boundaries and knew precisely when to assert himself. The raw authenticity of individuals unafraid to challenge norms resonated with her, creating a magnetic pull toward those who embraced their true, untamed selves.

Just then, their study session was abruptly disrupted by Corvus attempting a daring aerial feat from the top of a bookshelf, only to crash headfirst into a pile of scrolled parchment, sending them scattering in every direction.

"Seems the captain's adventures have encountered a bit of turbulence," Asher quipped, a smirk playing on his lips. They observed Corvus, with its feathers slightly askew but undetermined, regain balance amidst the fluttering papers.

Herodotus, having been startled awake by the commotion, stretched to its full length, and began to groom itself, unperturbed by the antics of the feathered visitor. The mechanical purr grew louder, filling the air with a soft, rhythmic hum.

"Quite the scholar," Asher remarked, gesturing toward Herodotus. "I often find Herodotus to be the epitome of leisure, even amidst the most arduous research."

Ruby smiled, admiring the contrast between the meticulously groomed cat and the raven's clumsiness. "Looks like Corvus is more interested in exploring than the historian is in educating." Their shared amusement echoed through the library, drawing irritated glances from nearby scholars trying to focus on their studies.

Mollie's arrival interrupted the lighthearted banter, her satin-heeled boots echoing across the library's wooden floors. "What's all this then?"

Ruby was helping Asher pick up the strewn scrolls, accidentally brushing her hand to his, paused, and quickly pointed up to Corvus perched precariously on a large wooden beam. "Just a little sky-high mischief, Mollie. I believe you're already acquainted with the captain."

Mollie eyed the raven with common amusement. "Why, yes. He certainly looks like he's gearing up for another daring flight."

A chuckle escaped Asher as he nodded in agreement, absently touching Ruby's freckled arm. "Seems like your friend here is destined for trouble, just like Herodotus," he laughed, casting a glance toward his cat, now venturing to a nearby stairwell. "Pleased to meet you, Mollie, is it?" He set down a bundle of scrolls and held out his hand, "I am a friend of Ruby's," he said, offering her a friendly wink.

"Delighted," she replied smugly, shaking his hand. "Excuse us," she said, grabbing Ruby's elbow and yanking her down an adjacent aisle. As Mollie and Ruby discussed Lavoie and their need for transportation, the atmosphere in the library changed.

The books on their right shifted slightly, and suddenly, Asher's curious face appeared between the volumes. "An airship. That's the best, and fastest, way to get to Egypt," he chimed in, sounding enthusiastic. "I've always dreamt of going there. Mind if I tag along?"

Mollie and Ruby shared a look, a silent conversation unfolding between them.

Just then, Corvus cawed softly, its eyes seemingly gleaming with interest. Meanwhile, Herodotus lounged gracefully upon an empty shelf, its tail flicking in apparent agreement with Asher's suggestion.

"An airship it is, then," Ruby said, turning to their pets. "Looks like you both have made your choice crystal clear."

Mollie's disbelief was palpable. Her eyes full of blue fire. She leaned in and whispered, "Are you barmy? We don't know anything about him." She pointed a finger at Ruby. "We are *not* bringing a total stranger with us," she snapped, crossing her arms, and turning away. "Forget him."

Could she? Could she forget the way she felt the first time he looked at her with those magnetizing eyes? Could she forget the way her blood sang in her veins when he touched her? When she went to Egypt, and England was far, far away, could she forget Asher Salt?

She didn't think so.

Ruby understood, perhaps better than Mollie, that thoughts fuel emotions and proceeded cautiously. "I understand your reservations," she said, trying to assuage her concerns, "but consider this: his expertise in ancient history and particularly Egypt could prove invaluable. Just think of it."

Mollie turned and faced Ruby, her mood lightening as she contemplated her words. She knew all too well about Ruby's stubbornness—she held onto things when they were important to her. And despite their close bond, Mollie understood that arguing with Ruby was often futile.

"Well, I—" Mollie began, but Ruby cut her off.

"Besides, traveling by ourselves might not be the safest choice," Ruby interjected.

"Fine. Have it your way. There's no point in arguing with the likes of you," Mollie retorted, still irritated. She closed her eyes, drew in a breath, and let it out with a slight huff. "What's the plan?"

"I'll go to Lavoie and accept the terms of his deal... but I have one important condition," she declared with faintest trace of mischief.

"What's that?" Asher inquired.

"He must give me the scarab amulet as collateral. Once I secure the scepter, I'll surrender both items. That way, our obligation is met, and we cut ties with Lavoie—forever."

8

The following morning, Ruby found herself once more outside Lavoie's Jewelry Emporium. A fleeting moment of hesitation gripped her as she paused at the door, her fingerless gloved hand resting on the cool brass handle. Doubt crept in, casting her into the shadows of uncertainty regarding the resolve from the previous night. Was she jeopardizing her friends' safety for her own selfish reasons? The enigmatic amulet, cryptic dreams, and the inexplicable scarab tattoo fueled her quest for answers, and Egypt, with its mystic allure, appeared to hold the key to unraveling those mysteries.

Ruby's gnawing curiosity won her over. With a firm decision made, a sense of fortitude steeled her nerves. She adjusted her posture, straightening her back, and decisively stepped into the shop.

A handsome couple, their elegance akin to a living painting against the backdrop of sparkling jewels and polished brass. The lady adorned an apple green bone-infused corset over an ivory-colored dress that exuded understated grace. Her companion, equally refined, donned tails, white spats, and cradled a tall hat. An attentive tuxedoed automaton, a newer version than the one from before, followed them discreetly, ready to assist if called upon.

As the couple leisurely perused the array of engagement rings, their whispered exchanges and gentle touches spoke volumes of their affection. Meanwhile, Ruby took on the guise of a casual shopper, her fingers delicately grazing the display case across from them. Her attention danced from one earring to another, feigning interest while secretly observing the couple's amorous interactions and subtly waiting for the opportune moment when either Lavoie would become available, or the couple would conclude their visit.

As the couple exited, a familiar French-accented voice cut through the air, disembodied yet commanding, seizing Ruby's attention. "Ah, Mademoiselle, a pleasure to see you again. Returning for a specific reason, perhaps?"

Maintaining her composure, she replied, "Indeed, Monsieur. No reminders necessary of our last encounter, but I come seeking answers this time."

Lavoie emerged from behind a paneled wall. He stood taller than she had remembered, dressed in a gold-striped shirt that caught the glint of the chandelier's light and a waistcoat the color of fresh blood. He smirked, "Curiosity seems to have found a new home within you, Ruby Blood. So, what questions do you have for me?"

Choosing her words carefully, she continued, "The scarab amulet—its power, its origins—I want information about its secrets."

Lavoie regarded Ruby's request with a piercing gaze. "Ah, the allure of the ancient mystique," he mused, steepling his fingers under his chin. "But chéri, you know as well as anyone that knowledge comes at a price. And yes, I may or may not possess information that might pique your interest." His gaze, unwavering, hinted at the depth of his knowledge yet veiled the extent of what he was willing to divulge.

Maintaining a staunch demeanor, Ruby countered, "Your knowledge is only as valuable as your discretion, Monsieur."

He chuckled softly, a glint of amusement in his eyes. "You play a dangerous game, mon chéri. I trust you understand the stakes."

Taking a measured breath, Ruby met his gaze directly. "Quite well. But rest assured, I am not one to give in so easily."

Then he shared, as much as he was willing to, the story behind the scarab amulet. He acquired it during a nighttime transaction with a foreign trader at the shipping docks. According to this relic man, the scarab amulet had passed through several hands, originating centuries ago from a Brit who claimed to have been gifted it. He alleged that an underground society took it from the tomb of Pharoah Aketankhen Neferet, known by many as the Pharaoh of the Scarlet Scarab.

"So, you knew about the amulet's power?" she questioned.

"No, not at all. The true potential of the amulet remained a mystery until your touch awakened its dormant energy," Lavoie explained. "Excusez-moi." He briefly stepped out of the room and then returned carrying a rosewood box. As he approached, a searing sensation akin to being marked by a red-hot iron pierced through Ruby's tattoo. She cupped the back of her neck and it felt hot to the touch.

"Legends speak of the scarlet scarab amulet's extraordinary ability to amplify the scepter's inherent power, creating an unparalleled force," Lavoie mused, his voice trailing off as he placed the box on the desk. "Should they ever merge," he continued, punctuating his words with a quick, emphatic clap of his hands for emphasis, "together."

After a dramatic and noticeable pause, he continued, "And now, for that coveted information... the price. Besides procuring the scarlet scarab scepter, you'll need to venture deep into Luxor's clandestine society. Unearth the concealed truths about the amulet and the scepter's combined capabilities—their true power and potential." There was an undeniable weight to his words, an expectation that hung in the air like a corrupt contract.

As Ruby gently unlatched the closure, a soft hiss accompanied the subtle quiver of tiny gears, unveiling the inner pouch. Red silk, as soft as a whisper, adorned the interior, cradling the scarlet scarab amulet within. Nestled in its cushioned recess, the amulet gleamed beneath a protective, transparent glass, captivating with its vibrant hues while assuring its safeguarding.

With that, the deal was sealed.

On Ruby's way back to the library, Lavoie's cryptic words reverberated within her thoughts like an ominous refrain: "Knowledge comes at a price." And it certainly did. Retrieving the scarlet scarab scepter was a formidable task on its own. Yet, now, this precarious pact—delving into Luxor's secret society—bore an unknowable price tag.

At the library, Ruby shared the details of Lavoie's proposition. Mollie and Asher's reactions were immediate—and a palpable sense of resistance and apprehension filled the air. Asher's furrowed brow mirrored Mollie's concern, both exchanging disconcerted glances.

Mollie broke the awkward silence. "How are we supposed to find a hidden scepter *and* infiltrate an underground society? This is a suicide mission," she declared, turning to Asher, seeking support, "Right?"

"Sorry. But I agree with Mollie. It sounds too risky." Asher shrugged his shoulders, giving Ruby an apologetic look.

Undeterred Ruby continued her train of thought, adding, "Our priority now is getting transportation—as Asher suggested, an airship, that's our best bet," attempting to find common ground amongst them. She held the folded map between her fingers, offering it as evidence. "Look—Lavoie gave me this map, marking several sites and the name of a curator who can help us," she added, trying to underscore the significance of the information obtained.

Mollie's disappointment was evident as she tutted softly to herself. "Really, is that all?" Her voice carried a note of bitterness.

"At least it's a starting point," Ruby added. What lingered between them as the realization dawned on her was that the map and Lavoie's contact might hold limited clues, leaving her once again with more questions than answers.

"At the *very* least," Mollie quipped. "Besides, we can't afford passage to Egypt. Did you even consider that?"

Ruby arched an eyebrow. Without saying a word, she unbuckled the leather bandolier secured around her waist. The pouch, carefully crafted to hold currency, bulged with banknotes.

They were both quiet after that.

As they left the library, Ruby glanced at Mollie and Asher, a spark of excitement lighting up her eyes. "I can't wait to uncover the mysteries of the scarlet scarab with you two by my side."

As the gears of their clockwork companions hummed softly, they stepped into the London evening, anticipation gleaming in their eyes and determination echoing in their footsteps.

9

Standing at the docks, a gentle breeze carried the crisp London air, tousling Ruby's copper curls as she gazed at the airship before her. Its polished brass and steel gleamed under the muted sunlight, casting a magnificent silhouette against the vast expanse of the sky. Its large, billowing sails adorned with elaborate mechanisms caught her eye, whispering tales of foreign destinations and grand adventures. Steam hissed rhythmically from its engines, and the hum of gears echoed softly, infusing the air with an industrial symphony beckoning them like a siren's song.

Ruby nudged Asher, her eyes brightening. "Look," she said, pointing to the airship. "That's our way to Egypt."

Asher followed her sightline and nodded. "Let's find out."

They hurried toward the ship where an imposing man with a rugged look and walrus mustache supervised the loading of crates onto the airship. His coat, adorned with various gadgets and trappings, exuded an air of authority.

"Excuse me," Ruby called out as they approached him. "Are you the captain of this vessel?"

The man pivoted, his piercing blue eyes scanning them with a hint of curiosity. "Tha' be me. Cap'ain Ambrose, a' yer service, missus," he greeted, tipping his cap.

As he extended his hand for a handshake, it was then that Ruby noticed something different—the glint of a brass prosthetic arm reaching out. She faltered for a moment, her discomfort evident, having not anticipated it until that very handshake. Yet, she quickly composed herself, returning the handshake with a friendly smile.

"Blood. Ruby Blood," she introduced herself, a hint of confidence in her voice.

"Aye, bricky young thing, ain' we? I'm obliged," he gruffly replied, clasping her hand with his prosthetic one.

The handshake resonated with an unexpected warmth that contrasted with the roughness of his grip.

"Asher Salt," he added, nodding swiftly.

Ambrose's gaze drifted to Mollie, his curiosity piqued. "Ye 'here, a baske' ov awanges ye are, who migh' ye be?"

She fidgeted. "Mollie," she answered hastily, turning her attention back to the airship avoiding his lingering gaze.

"Where migh' ye youngsters be 'eading?" Ambrose inquired, his Cockney accent giving a melodious flair to his words. "Sky's de limi,'" he chuckled, his laughter carrying a sense of adventure, akin to the endless expanse of the skies above them.

"We're looking for passage to Egypt," Ruby said, urgency coloring her voice, "right away."

"Egyp'?" Ambrose removed his cap and scratched his head. "Migh' be a bi' ov a stre'ch," he muttered. Affectionately patting the hull, then he added, "Ye see, she's still in 'he wawks. Righ' away migh' be stre'chin i' a wee bi' 'oo far."

"I am willing to offer additional compensation," Ruby offered, hoping to pique his interest.

Ambrose raised an eyebrow and twirled the end of his mustache, his intrigue evident. "Well, don' leave me 'angin. Wha' are ye offerin'?"

As Ruby unraveled their plan, Captain Ambrose leaned in, his gaze attentive, nodding occasionally in acknowledgment. "Short on time and in need of a reliable means to reach our destination and return swiftly," she emphasized, holding up a small, tightly knotted velvet pouch filled with gold bullion. The jangle of the bright coins underscored her urgency.

Ambrose stroked his mustache, weighing the proposition. "I's a risky ven'ure, bu' my ship's de bes' ye go' in 'his whole shipyard." His gaze met Ruby's. "Ye go' a deal, Miss Blood, bu' under one condi'ion." Ruby held her breath, anticipating his terms. "We leave a' dawn. No excep'ions," Captain Ambrose laughed a hearty laugh that reverberated off the hull.

She nodded in agreement, relieved. "Then dawn it shall be."

Afterward, the three of them strolled to a nearby tavern known as The Copper Finch, a renowned establishment favored by airship crews. The place exuded an old-world charm, a fusion of comfortable leather and smoky shadows. Deep green hues enveloped the walls, adorned with rows of vintage airship parts and intriguing trinkets, casting an inviting amber glow across the establishment.

Inside, the air was filled with melodies emanating from an opulent phonograph. Its steel pipes and valves produced rich, warm sounds amplified through an ornate speaker. A fine-tipped cogwheel traced the record grooves, while the brass instrument stood prominently at the heart of the tavern.

As they settled in at a round table, the tavern buzzed with conversation, card games, and the clinking of glasses. Behind the bar, a bartender polished a row of hobnail tumblers, and the air carried the sweet scent of aged bourbon and rich, earthy cigars.

Engaged in conversation with Ruby and Mollie, Asher's attention darted back and forth between the girls and a rugged figure, shrouded in a weathered leather duster, who sat conspicuously across from them at the bar. What caught Asher's immediate attention, however, was the ocular apparatus affixed to the man's left eye, emitting a subtle, faint glow amidst the dimly lit surroundings.

Suddenly, the man slammed his drink down onto the bar's surface, the crack of his neck audible as he began to saunter purposefully toward Asher's table. The brass and copper adornments of his ocular apparatus shimmered as it rotated, an intimidating reflection of his harsh nature, much like the revolver conspicuously hanging at his side, a silent testament to his uncompromising demeanor.

With an ogling stare fixed on Ruby, he leaned down close to her ear, a wicked smirk crossing his face as whiskey and trouble seemed to emanate from his pores. "Alrigh,' red. Le's 'ave us a 'urn round 'he dance floaw."

Taking care not to meet his eye, she said, "No," and then added politely, "Thank you." She brought a small glass of amber-colored liquid up to her lips.

"I don' 'ake kindly 'hearin no—come on."

Asher reacted swiftly, springing to his feet with a suddenness that belied his usual calm demeanor. His body tensed, muscles coiling like a tightly wound spring, as his hands clenched into fists at his sides. With a steely resolve, he fixed his gaze upon the man before him, his eyes ablaze with a fierce determination.

"Wha's 'hat, boy," he grunted. He turned his face to a nearby table of men playing dice. "Lad's go' 'to be soddenin' d'unk," he snorted.

"Listen here, mate, she's with me," Asher interjected firmly, extending his hand to Ruby. "Come on, love."

Ruby's eyes widened, caught between surprise and uncertainty, as the tension in the air crackled with Asher's protective gesture. Before Ruby could even form a response or react, the man's hand reached out, aiming for her elbow.

Before his touch landed, Asher's voice thundered through the air, laced with palpable defiance. "Back off! She's not interested, especially not with a gibface like you!" His words cut through the tense atmosphere, a declaration of protection and a firm warning all wrapped into one.

The man withdrew his arm, cocked his head, and his lip curled into a cold, calculating sneer. "I'm gonna rip yer 'ongue ou' by de roots—*hero*," he snarled, his fingers paddling the steel of his revolver.

Suddenly, the man lunged, aiming to grab Asher, but Asher, being younger and quicker, deftly dodged his grasp with an agile sidestep. The ensuing chaos unfolded as a table crashed, chairs toppled, and the room reverberated with shouts.

Asher moved with remarkable agility, navigating through the chaotic scene like a prizefighter, effortlessly evading the blows thrown in his direction. With swift and precise movements, he disarmed the blackguard, skillfully defusing the threat and guiding him out of the door without inflicting harm.

The crowd erupted into cheers, impressed by Asher's display of prowess and finesse amidst the brawl. As the dust settled and the echoes of the commotion faded, Asher returned to their table, a smile played across his lips. "Sorry about that, ladies," he said, settling back into his seat and picking up his drink. The remnants of adrenaline lingered in his voice as he spoke, his tone carrying a touch of humility despite the admiration he had garnered.

Mollie elbowed him playfully. "That was really something. You gave that git a run for his money."

Despite his anger only moments ago, there was now something like pride shining in his eyes. The bartender swept past their table, offering Asher a nod of approval. He shrugged, a faint blush gracing his cheeks. "Oh, that was nothing, just had to defuse the situation, is all."

Ruby's eyes locked with his and she couldn't help but smile, grateful for his courage and quick thinking. "Guess he was right, you are quite the hero," she remarked, admiringly.

As the evening progressed, the ambient sounds of chatter and clinking glasses enveloped the trio once more. They delved into deep discussions, contemplating the risks and myriad of possibilities that lay ahead on their impending adventure. And when they bid each other goodnight and went their separate ways, an emblem of inner elation surged through Ruby. Anticipation pulsed through her veins, entwined with a heavy dose of something more than friendship towards Asher—a budding sense of romantic intrigue.

The morning sun was partially obscured behind a curtain of white clouds as they headed toward the docks. The air buzzed with anticipation, and the distant clanging of machinery echoed across the bustling port. There, towering proudly, was Captain Ambrose's airship, a splendid creation, its massive mahogany propellers dull in the dim morning light.

Standing on deck, Ambrose adjusted his goggles while inspecting the airship's outward mechanisms. Silver gadgets dangled from his toolbelt. His brass compass, etched with gears and filigree, shimmered with an iridescent glow. Tiny gears spun within, guiding the needle to true north. Crowned with a glass dome, the compass protected a mesmerizing gyroscopic mechanism that softly hummed.

"Mo'nin'!" Ambrose's voice boomed. "Ready de se' sail?" he asked, lighting a wooden pipe, releasing wispy circles of white smoke in the air.

"All set, captain!" Ruby replied, her voice carrying a hint of excitement. Corvus soared above the mast, circled it, and gracefully landed on it. Ruby's gaze shifted to Asher, a subtle glimmer of anticipation and something more passing between them. The air buzzed with a sense of adventure as they readied themselves to embark on their journey together.

10

The airship rose steadily, its ascent smooth and graceful. Aside from its functionality, the airship was a sight to behold. Ornate brass fittings lined the polished wooden rails, catching the sunlight in dazzling flashes. Grand mechanisms whirred and clicked, orchestrating the dance of gears and pulleys that kept the vessel aloft. The inflated balloon, buoyant with the promise of smooth travel, cast a majestic silhouette against the clear blue sky.

As the airship soared, Ruby experienced a whirlwind of emotions—an exhilarating yet nerve-wracking sensation—as the security of solid ground slipped away beneath her feet. She watched as London transformed into miniature landscapes. The cityscape dwindled, the grand buildings shrinking into tiny structures, and the bustling streets narrowed into dark, thin, tangled ribbons snaking through the vastness below.

Asher looked at Mollie and chuckled. "You're looking quite pale. Nervous?"

With a nervous grin, Mollie replied, her fingers tracing a line on the edge of her cobalt waistcoat. "Of course. It's just quite the leap, isn't it?" She took a deep breath and slowly exhaled. "I don't much like having my feet so far off the ground is all."

Sitting on a rail, Corvus let out a loud squawk, causing Herodotus to swat with a playful paw, momentarily distracting Mollie from her weak stomach. Corvus's eyes gleamed as his head bobbed and weaved, a mechanical dance of anticipation, while Herodotus performed an acrobatic leap to dodge a playful peck.

At the helm, Ambrose let out a hearty chuckle. "Never fear, Miss Mollie! Cawvus and 'erodotus are season'd adven'urers. 'hey'll see ye 'hrough."

Mollie's gaze blinked between the mischievous raven and the curious feline, finding a small measure of comfort in their entertaining antics. "Right. Friends in high places, then," she said with a faint smile.

Ambrose interjected with a soothing tone. "A leap in'o 'he unknown, Miss Mollie. Bu' fear no', adven'ure beckons!"

Asher grinned. "Besides, where's the fun without a bit of uncertainty, eh?" He gave Mollie an encouraging pat on the back.

The airship thrummed with vitality, almost like a sentient creature, its sails unfurling proudly as if responding to the eager winds. The woven network of ropes pulled tautly, crisscrossed like veins across its expansive frame. Each metallic hum and subtle creaking of greased cogwheels created a smooth blend of nature and machine. It was more than just a vessel—it seemed to lurch and pulsate with a sense of purpose, as if longing to embark on another thrilling voyage through the skies.

At the helm, within the transparent portion of the wheel, a glowing blue luminescence sloshed, swirling violently as Ambrose spun it. His prosthetic arm, a marvel of practical ingenuity, seamlessly attached to the wheel, its gears and plungers mirroring the ship's movements, adding a touch of mechanical elegance to his commanding presence.

"Bu' de hea' ov 'his Levia'han resides in de engine room."

"May we see it?" Ruby asked.

"Follah me." Disconnecting his prosthetic arm, he bounded down the stairs two at a time, leading them to the engine room. As they descended deep into the belly of the airship, the rhythmic chugging of the engine grew angrier, the metallic growling resonating throughout the entire room.

"Behold!" Ambrose announced proudly, his hands out wide gesturing toward a massive, precisely crafted engine. "Every gear, knob, an' lever plays a key role in 'er opera'ion."

The interior chamber was a testament to industrial ingenuity, a masterpiece resembling a metallic heart, pulsing with energy, its rhythmic throbbing syncing with the airship's movements. The air, filled with the soft whir of machinery and the aroma of grease and oil, created an atmosphere steeped in both power and efficiency.

As the airship glided through the skies the rhythmic hum of the engine blended in seamlessly with the soft rattling gears. Given that there was little air traffic and favorable weather, the journey took a little less than four days traversing at a high rate of speed. The airship cut easily through the white clouds, cruising over varied landscapes—rolling hills, dense forests, and wide rivers that snaked across the land like giant glistening serpents.

The girls' cabin walls boasted wallpaper adorned with bird-in-flight patterns, each delicate feather meticulously gilded, giving the compact quarter an air of refined sophistication. Positioned near the kitchen, the aroma of wood smoke lingered, mingling pleasantly with the tantalizing scents of roast pork and Brown Windsor soup.

Most evenings, Mollie, nestled in a corner of the cabin, dove into her journals, the faint glow of a brass-shaded lamp illuminating the pages. She scribbled notes in sepia ink, capturing the nuances of the ever-changing landscapes below. Beside her, a small astrolabe clicked softly, aiding her in recording the positions and celestial markers that guided their journey.

In the snug confines of their cabin, Asher would visit. They spent evenings regaling each other with tales, laughter, and the occasional teasing that they fondly referred to as 'playful banter.'

A small, purring motor stood behind Asher's favorite lounging chair, contributing a soothing rhythm to their conversations. The wall-mounted clock's hands moved with metronome-like precision, marking time well spent in the cozy space with Asher.

"I still can't believe you pinched that diamond," Asher teased playfully.

Ruby laughed, her eyes sparkling. "Well, I couldn't let that one slip by, could I? Besides, it was just sitting there, begging to be taken." Her laughter bubbled up.

Shaking his head with an affectionate smile, as the tiny mechanisms in his onyx cufflinks swirled and glinted in the cabin light, he laughed. "You really are a rogue."

With a mischievous glint in her eye, she said, "I'll admit, my pursuits are a bit unconventional, but they do make life more exciting, don't they?"

"You know," he murmured, drawing nearer, "there's a world beyond larceny." For the first time, Asher consciously pondered how Ruby had come to embrace this criminal profession, surrounded by gleaming riches and daring thieving intent. But he refrained from delving deeper into the matter—for now, at least. Picking up a lock of her hair, he lingered a moment, twirling the strand around his finger before tucking it behind her ear with a tender smile.

"Suggesting a career change, are we?" she quipped, raising an eyebrow.

"That I am and a proper one too. You're not just clever—you're brilliant, love," he murmured, his hand closing over hers. His words hung in the air.

Ruby didn't know how to be anything other than what she was. A thief. She always embraced the shadows, weaving through the labyrinth of secrets and deceit. Yet, in those moments with Asher, a glimmer of something more beckoned—chance for redemption or a new beginning.

Night after night, as they delved deeper into their conversations, the gears of dialogue turned effortlessly, smoothly transitioning from one topic to the next. Their discussions revealed a symphony of thoughts and passions, igniting a profound understanding between them, sparking something deeper—a silent understanding that transcended the limited time they had spent getting to know each other.

Their shared moments became more than just conversations. They were the tender threads of an unbreakable bond growing stronger with each passing word, each fleeting smile, and each stolen glance.

11

Asher was perceptive, adept at unraveling the layers Ruby tried to hide. As he spoke, his narrative meandered through personal anecdotes about his father, a distinguished professor of anthropology whose passion for all things ancient had deeply influenced Asher. It was through these tales that his fascination with history took root. His eyes lit up as he described the history of ancient artifacts and the secrets held within them, painting a vivid picture of his passionate pursuit of knowledge.

"I can't seem to find the exact page right now," he said, flipping through the pages. His eyes sparkled with a hint of excitement as he rifled through a series of small leatherback volumes, searching for the specific passage he had marked for reference. "But the stories surrounding these artifacts often carry a kernel of truth. Legends like these, well they might be rooted in some ancient beliefs or events."

Ruby leaned closer, drawn in by his enthusiasm, and caught a faint scent of cloves and cinnamon. "You can't recall the details, the ones about the Scarlet Scarab Pharaoh?" Her curiosity surged, hungry for any scrap of information that might reveal the mysteries surrounding the scarlet scarab.

"No, it was a small part of a larger context, a mere snippet from a historical text," he explained, still looking through his books. "Something about a curse."

"A curse?" she laughed amusedly. You're not suggesting you believe in such things, are you? Next, you'll be telling me ghosts are real and Loch Ness too."

"Well, I do know that relics can have influence on those who encounter them. You might've simply been reacting to the amulet's mystical aura, not necessarily a curse," he offered, scholarly skepticism fortifying his words.

"The dreams and the tattoo came before I ever laid eyes on the amulet, and when I touched it, I felt its power," she explained.

"Perhaps there's a missing piece, an answer hidden in the amulet's history or the tombs themselves. We'll figure it out," he declared, and then added, "together."

In Asher, Ruby found a refreshing departure from the familiar script of fleeting connections and superficial encounters. His genuine interest in navigating challenges together spoke volumes. She appreciated not only the warmth of his smile but also the depth behind his gaze—an unspoken understanding that transcended mere physical attraction. She couldn't help but feel a sense of gratitude for the unexpected connection that was rewriting the narrative of her romantic experiences.

One especially clear evening, a casual touch meant to steady themselves during sudden turbulence became a moment that changed everything—for them, forever. While on deck discussing conspicuous constellations of creatures in the sky, the airship shuddered violently. Instinctively Asher's arm wrapped around Ruby's waist. A rush of warmth surged through her at his touch, igniting a firestorm of emotions.

Their gazes locked. Asher's sultry eyes sparkled, making her breathless. Ruby's heart thundered, its rapid rhythm adding to the dizzying intensity of the moment. His hand caught hers, sending an electric pulse through her fingertips.

He leaned in, his breath a whisper against the fronds of her hair. Ruby turned toward him, their faces drawing closer until his lips softly met hers. It was an unexpected embrace, but within that fleeting moment, a delicious languor washed over her senses—the warmth of his lips, the gentle tug of his hands in her hair, drawing her closer in a tight embrace. An invisible link formed between them, an intimacy that transcended the physical. Her face lingered in the sheltering curve of his shoulder until he raised her chin and claimed her lips again.

And again.

A magnetic current seemed to flow between them, setting every nerve singing with love and awareness.

Since they first met, Asher's thoughts and dreams had revolved around Ruby: her hair as red as roses, her eyes as green as priceless emeralds. He found himself captivated by her—the subtle curve of her mouth, or lack of curve, revealing her moods. Her wit and intelligence sparked a fire in his soul, igniting a sense of admiration and fascination that he had never experienced before.

Finally, the following day, the airship loomed over Egypt. As they approached the raised landing platform, they gathered at the bow of the airship, excited by the breathtaking sight below. The sprawling expanse of desert stretched out before them, the hot midday sun casting a warm glow upon the dunes that rippled like ocean currents stuck in time.

"All 'ands on deck! Prepare for landin', ye cloud 'oppers!" Ambrose announced, his voice loud and clear.

Ruby felt a renewed ambition as the world was growing larger by the day. She leaned against the railing, her eyes tracing the contours of the approaching landscape. "It's splendid!"

Leaning in, Asher cupped her cheek in his hand. "And we'll get answers here," he remarked. "I promise." She lifted her chin, locked her eyes with him, and smiled.

Mollie squinted, peering into the horizon. "I'm glad it's still daylight. Looks like we've got awhile before sunset."

Ambrose guided the airship toward the designated landing area, a patch of open desert bordered by weathered ruins and the distant silhouette of the Nile River. The airship slowly descended, the engines whirring as the ground grew closer and closer.

"Brace yourselves, land luvers!" Ambrose shouted, his hands deftly maneuvering the huge rudder and secondary controls.

The airship descended gracefully, its massive weight pressing down as the landing gear made contact with the ground. The sand billowed in a whirlwind around the airship, caught in the powerful downdraft. Then with a soft thud, the craft settled in, and the engines powered down, their hum fading into the warm desert breeze.

"Finally!" Mollie exclaimed, relieved to be once again on solid ground.

Herodotus trotted ahead, leading the way down the gangplank. "Let's go," Asher said, with a girl on each arm.

Ambrose, still at the helm, tipped his cap and shouted down to them. "Be careful, me hearties, in de bleedin' desert an' de tales it weaves," he shared, his eyes sparkling with the spirit of adventure. He exchanged a salute and a knowing smile with Captain Corvus, still perched atop the ship's mast, its mechanical wings fluttering in farewell.

Herodotus, gleaming in the sunlight, ambled through the sand toward an adjacent tent. The tent's canvas, a tawny hue reminiscent of sun-drenched parchment, bore a weathered and coarse texture, evidence of the relentless desert winds and sand wearing it down.

Near the landing platform, they were each given the same mode of transport—an extraordinary breed of camels, far from the usual humped creatures. These camels were adorned with rubberized accoutrements that emitted soft bouts of steam, and distressed harnesses embellished with colorful tassels and mini cowrie shells.

"Are you sure about this?" Mollie whispered, eyeing the camels warily. "They look like they belong in a blooming parade, not a desert trek."

Ruby nodded, sharing her concern. "I know, but it seems like we don't have much choice. Let's hope they're as reliable as they look."

12

The relentless sun beat down upon the vast expanse of desert, its scorching rays turning the sand into a sea of shimmering gold. Ruby adjusted her grip on the camel's jangling reins, squinting against the blinding light as she surveyed their surroundings. The air was thick with the heat of midday, mirages dancing on the horizon like elusive specters. Turning to Asher, who was busy adjusting the straps on his camel's harness, Ruby spoke up, her voice barely audible over the desert wind. "Asher, where to Luxor or Cairo?"

Asher paused, his brow furrowing in thought as he considered their options. "Map marked Luxor. The Valley of the Kings," he replied finally, his voice tinged with determination.

"Isn't the Egyptologist Lavoie mentioned working inside Luxor Temple's Museum?" Mollie interjected.

"Yes, Octavia Thorne. I've read about her," Asher replied, scooping up Herodotus, his tone reflective. "She's got her finger on the pulse of Egypt's archaeological sites," he continued, mounting his camel with ease. "She's quite renowned in her field, known for her meticulous research and groundbreaking discoveries."

"Perfect. Maybe she can help me unravel this scarab mystery," Ruby said. "And help us find that blasted scepter."

Mollie adjusted herself on the camel, a thoughtful expression on her face. "I certainly hope so. We can use all the help we can get."

Asher turned to the guide. "Sir, to Luxor."

The camels grunted and groaned, their long-riveted necks clanging and creaking as they obediently pulled the camels in the correct direction.

Just outside of Luxor, they traversed past a vibrant marketplace. It was a tapestry of kaleidoscopic colors and fervent activity, where merchants hawked their goods and umbrella-toting tourists sauntered amidst the lively scene

—creating a mesmerizing scene against the pale windswept ancient edifices.

Luxor Temple stood tall, an architectural marvel. Its façade boasted six colossal stone pillars, embellished with carved hieroglyphs. In the bustling streets near the temple, individuals paraded in sheath dresses, wraparound kilts, and other eclectic attire. Some wielded brass contraptions—pocket-sized wind gauges and telescopic goggles—while others boasted automatons that served as tour guides.

Within the lively cityscape of Luxor, the most awe-inspiring spectacle was the presence of elephants gracefully parading through the bustling streets. These colossal creatures, adorned with elaborate motorized enhancements, served as both majestic transports for passengers and goods. Their grand steel joints creaked rhythmically as they lumbered through the dust-laden streets.

Venturing into the museum portion of the temple, a treasure trove of ancient artifacts awaited exploration. Glass cases displayed artifacts dating back thousands of years. These priceless relics were paired with state-of-the-art informational displays, featuring intricate clockwork models and vibrant absinthe-green projections that elucidated their historical significance.

"Look at this!" Mollie exclaimed, her finger tracing the outline of a symbol in the shape of a cross with a distinctive loop at its top.

Leaning over the display, Asher said, "That's an ankh. It symbolizes life, bridging the realms between the living and the dead," he said in a mocking spooky voice. He pointed. "See here, it says that some pharaohs even had 'ankh' in their names."

"Like Pharaoh Aketankhen," Mollie quipped.

Asher smiled. "Indeed. It's a powerful Egyptian symbol."

"Sort of looks like a key," Ruby remarked, finding a curious connection to her line of work in this ancient relic.

Asher nodded in agreement. "Yes." He gestured to a suspended glowing projection revealing this very detail. "See here. It's known as the 'key of life'."

They continued moving quickly through the narrow corridors, perusing the exhibitions, and trying to locate anyone who might point them in Octavia Thorne's direction. Flickering light from gaslit sconces cast undulating shadows along the painted stone walls, mirroring the rhythmic movements depicted in the ancient scenes steeped in traditional rituals.

When they reached the jewelry exhibition chamber, Mollie and Asher looked casually and walked on, but Ruby's eyes gleamed with a mixture of curiosity and mischief. One display in particular captured her interest. It held an array of gold jewelry—a collection of rare pieces, each telling a story of archaic craftsmanship and prodigious wealth.

Waiting for a break in the crowd, Ruby, once alone, with a practiced hand and a keen eye for opportunity, extracted a hairpin from underneath her vibrant curls.

Carefully, she inserted it into the case's lock, a simple mechanism, with a deft twist and a soft pop, the case yielded to her skillful manipulation. She removed a gold bracelet which bore petite gemstones from its stand. Reaching into her waistcoat's pocket, she took out a polished gold bangle—a piece nicked from an earlier heist. With a swift and practiced motion, she swapped the ancient bracelet for the modern one and locked the case. She cradled the bracelet within her palm, emitting a single click with her tongue.

In response, Corvus drifted into the chamber and silently perched atop her shoulder. Talons grasped the bracelet, concealing it within a hidden compartment beneath its breast in mere seconds. But, in the swift motion, the razor-sharp talons scraped the top of Ruby's hand eliciting a loud shriek that caught Asher's attention as he stood near the corridor of the room.

Asher was at Ruby's side in an instant, quickly assessing the cut, concern drawn across his face. His eyes darted around, and spotting a nearby table, he swiftly grabbed a handkerchief from his pocket, deftly folding it into a makeshift bandage. With gentle yet sure movements, he wrapped the handkerchief around her hand, securing it in place to stem the bleeding.

"You got blood on you," she said. Just then, her hand flew to her neck where the tattoo was. It burned hot to the touch and just as quickly subsided, like a fleeting flame flickering against her skin.

"So, I did," he acknowledged, rubbing the streak of blood off. "No worries, love." A brief kiss on her hand followed, an instinctive gesture of reassurance and care.

As Ruby's pain subsided, they merged back into the flow of visitors, rejoining Mollie, the incident, barely a ripple in the bustling scene around them.

While Ruby stood among an exhibit of scepters, a sudden movement caught her attention, and for a fleeting moment, there he was—she could see his reflection in the mirror. Behind her, close, lurked a hooded figure shrouded within a shadowy cloak. She whirled around, scanning the area for any sign of the elusive figure, hoping that someone else had noticed. But no one appeared to have. The air was thick with curiosity and a hint of unease as the visitors continued their exploration, unaware of the mysterious encounter that had just transpired.

Could it truly be the same man, all the way there from London? Ruby's mind raced with possibilities. Or, even more worrying, could there be others, sent by Luxor's secret society, the one Lavoie had mentioned? The temple's dimly lit corridors seemed to hide a myriad of secrets, amplifying Ruby's unease.

Without warning, a flurry of motion caught Ruby's eye, drawing her immediate attention. A black cat, sleek in ruthenium and adorned with a gold broad collar, leg cuffs, and earrings, darted across the floor. It moved with an eerie semblance of life, its eyes glinting with spectral intelligence. With uncanny grace, it slinked toward Asher, low on its haunches, its tail swishing rapidly in a rhythmic pattern.

Herodotus emerged from Asher's satchel with an abrupt hiss. The sudden sound startled Corvus, perched atop a stone pedestal, causing it to swiftly unfurl its wings casting an eerie shadow over the unfolding scene below.

"Bastet, begone!" a voice scolded. An elegantly garbed woman came into view. She was extremely handsome with dark hair swept up in a mass of braids and ringlets, almond-shaped eyes dark and lively framed by a thick fringe of lashes. She wore a Spencer coat of burgundy silk and a pearl-laced corset platted along the side but most notably, she donned a pair of taupe trousers —trousers, a choice both shocking and extraordinary in the context of women's fashion.

"Smashing!" Ruby said absently, her cheeks flushed. "Apologies. You—"

Mollie interrupted, "You must be Ms. Thorne. Right?"

Before the woman could respond, Asher let out a deafening scream, clenching his hands into white-knuckled fists that suddenly darkened to a deep shade akin to charcoal. The chalky darkness bled upward along his wrists and arms, resembling ink dispersing in water.

Just then, thin red lines snaked up Asher's arms like veins of dark energy, gradually fading into the rest of his complexion. He fought to speak, his disbelief tangible, until the spreading darkness choked out his words. Tears welled in his eyes, mirroring the terror of the moment, just as his body collapsed to the ground, convulsing violently.

13

Bastet continued its slow advance toward Asher's trembling form. Each movement seemed calculated, deliberate, as if the creature were orchestrating the very convulsions wracking Asher's body. A rhythmic series of clicks emitted from its twitching whiskers and tail, synchronized with his spasms, creating an eerie symphony of dread. Corvus, still perched nearby, observed the scene with a chilling intensity, its eyes gleaming with an otherworldly glow that seemed to pierce through the darkness.

Meanwhile, Herodotus let out several loud, bellowing howls in a rapid, unsettling rhythm, adding to the palpable sense of fear that hung thick in the air. The museum's once serene atmosphere had transformed into a realm of terror, each click and movement amplifying the sense of impending doom. As Ruby watched, her heart pounded in her chest, her instincts screaming at her to flee. But she stood her ground, paralyzed by a mixture of fascination and dread, as the enigmatic forces at play unfolded before her eyes.

"Ladies, follow me," the woman commanded. "Quickly," the woman insisted, her voice a steely command.

At that, an imposing pair of jackal-headed Anubis guards approached Asher, their mechanical limbs moving with precision as they lifted him effortlessly. His body, now limp and unresponsive, seemed like a mere puppet in their formidable grasp. The harsh rhythmic echoes of their footsteps resonated down the long, dimly lit hallway, reverberating through the cavernous space.

"Ladies," the woman commanded with authority. "Quickly," she insisted, her voice carrying a steely resolve. Ruby's heart raced as she watched the guards carry Asher away, a sense of urgency gripping her.

"Come on," Mollie whispered affectionately, "Ruby, Ruby Red," her nickname yanking Ruby back to reality.

Together, they followed the woman down dimly lit corridors, passing rows of carved slab fragments that seemed to whisper secrets of ancient times. Softly glowing inventions adorned the walls, casting an ambient hue along their path. Ruby's mind raced with questions—What was happening to Asher? And what other terrible secrets awaited them yearning to be unveiled?

She stopped at a large wooden door, its black iron hinges creaking softly as the woman manipulated a small, ubiquitous rotary panel. A series of tumblers and pneumatic valves clicked into synchronized place under her practiced fingers. Inside, a laboratory filled with ancient artifacts and modern apparatuses—whirring gadgets, skeletal fragments, and cabinets with drawers spilling straw sat alongside scattered papers and strewn volumes.

"Ladies, pay heed. What you've just witnessed is the dreaded Curse of the Scarlet Scarab," she began, her voice regal and serious, as she surveyed them both. "I am Octavia Thorne, curator of this museum."

"Where did they take Asher?" Ruby blurted out. "Will he be, okay?"

Octavia's expression remained composed, though a hint of concern flickered in her eyes. "He is being cared for. The curse has been unleashed, and there's only one way that could have happened—but now, we must find a way to contain its power before it escalates beyond our control."

"Unleashed? How?" Ruby asked, her voice edged with a mix of disbelief and fear.

"Which of you—who's blood did he touch?" Her eyes darted between them, scanning for any telltale signs.

"Mine," Ruby confessed, her voice trembling slightly. "Just moments ago, I-I cut my hand." She held up her bandaged hand as proof, her gaze pleading for reassurance. "There's a cure, right?"

Octavia sighed, her voice gentle, like she was explaining something to a child. "The curse was transferred when he touched *your* blood. If anyone else, touches *your* blood, they will be infected too." She began searching inside a leather valise. "Have you any gloves?"

"My blood?" she said absently, and then replied, "Um, no." She shook her head, feeling the burden of responsibility settling on her shoulders.

"Here you are." She handed Ruby a pair of leather gloves, ecru in color and crafted from supple sheepskin embedded with copper-colored ankhs. As Ruby hurriedly slipped on the gloves, their snug fit offered a sense of reassurance.

"I-I didn't know," she whispered, feeling a mix of trepidation and regret.

"We know," Mollie said, her voice a comforting anchor.

Ruby's cheeks flushed. "Hold on," she murmured, gently sweeping the soft tangle of curls aside to reveal the red scarab tattoo etched on her skin. "Look," she said, pointing. The heat started to spread down her neck, illuminating her tattoo like a flashing beacon. "This tattoo —it appeared the morning after my seventeenth birthday."

"Did you say seventeenth?" She rubbed her chin thoughtfully. "Hmm, well, that is interesting... seventeen was the age the Scarlet Scarab Pharaoh met his untimely demise." Octavia's voice held a tinge of intrigue as she spoke.

From her pocket, she retrieved and unfurled a gold-framed lorgnette adorned with a telescopic lens. Leaning in, she scrutinized the markings closely, her expression transitioning from astonishment to an abrupt realization. "It's unmistakable," she continued. "This mark is a clear indication—" she paused, locking eyes with Ruby. "The Scarlet Scarab Curse has chosen its bearer." It was as if the echoes of history had resurfaced, tying Ruby's age to that of the ill-fated pharaoh, marking her as its chosen recipient. But why?

Sensing a tingling sensation beneath her skin, Ruby murmured, "It's been haunting my dreams. When I touched the scarab amulet, it was electrifying, and now Asher—I-I don't understand." Her voice wavered as she struggled to hold back tears. "Can we see him?"

Octavia's gaze remained on the tattoo. "Not yet. I assure you his needs are being met. This curse symbolizes a significant legacy, deeply tied to an ancient power. I need to gather my resources quickly. We'll leave within the hour," she declared firmly. "I know someone who I believe can help your friend."

Outside the temple was an armor-plated sand crawler outfitted with colossal tires, pneumatic suspension, and a periscope rising from its frame. Its sand displacement system featured a pair of sizable rotating blades, ensuring smooth passage through the ever-changing dunes.

To combat the intense sun, Ruby flipped a switch on her goggles, switched to her darkest lens, and inquired, "Where to?"

The sand crawler started with a severe jolt. "I have an associate whom I trust can help. Time is against us, and your friend's life hangs on a precarious edge!" Octavia's urgent words were almost lost in the engine's roar.

Before them, the desert stretched endlessly, a surging sea of golden sands that seemed to ripple like waves in the searing sun. The sun's ruthless glare turned the desert into a realm of illusions, mirages dancing on the edges of their vision—a trick that toyed with their weary eyes.

As the great wheels churned beneath them, they ventured deeper and deeper into the desert, an unshakable sense of unease lingering in the ardent air, conjuring haunting familiarity to Ruby's dreams. Corvus, with wings outstretched, soared above them, its wings sliced through the shimmering heat, casting elongated shadows across the dunes below.

Octavia remained focused, her goggled eyes scanning the vast distance, navigating only by memory. Meanwhile Ruby and Mollie shielded their faces from the sun, occasionally glancing at the horizon in search of any semblance of life.

But there was nothing.

"We're here!" Octavia exclaimed, bringing the sand crawler to an abrupt stop.

"Here?" Ruby said, gripping the rail, she stood up and took in the scene: an endless stretch of sand spreading to the horizon.

Mollie bounded out of the sand crawler, her baffled expression mirroring Ruby's uncertainty. "There's just sand... and more sand!" she exclaimed, frustration tinting her voice.

Octavia's enigmatic smile hinted at concealed insights. "Appearances can indeed deceive. Listen closely." She gestured for them to stay silent, placing a finger to her lips.

In the hushed stillness that followed, the air seemed to hum with an otherworldly energy. Ruby strained her ears, catching a distant yet distinct sound. It was a melodic resonance, a harmonious blend of ancient echoes and modern cadence. As the notes intertwined, a subtle vibration echoed around them, causing the very air to pulsate with an inexplicable force.

"What is that?" Mollie whispered, her eyes widening with a mixture of awe and confusion.

14

Octavia produced a cylinder embossed with red scarabs from her valise, its surface intricately adorned. With practiced finesse, she manipulated the device through a series of twists and turns in various directions, unveiling its concealed mechanism. From it, a wide pink arch of light appeared. Bending down, she placed the device onto the sand and ground it into the soft grains to stabilize it.

Within the rosy haze, a cityscape gradually emerged, teeming with life. The scene unfolded with intricate details, showcasing people going about their day in a busy town square.

"Follow me," Octavia said, striding confidently toward the aura.

"In there?" Mollie's voice wavered with uncertainty. "Not blooming likely!"

Octavia's smile was reassuring as she strode confidently into the cityscape. Ruby shrugged and followed, with Mollie reluctantly bringing up the rear.

Once inside, the pink haze and the desert heat dissipated, replaced by a refreshing cool breeze carrying the aroma of freshly baked bread. They found themselves standing amidst a cobblestone street adorned with vibrant blooms in bold colors, in stark contrast with the black wrought iron spires piercing the cloudless blue sky.

Octavia's assured steps guided them through the enchanting, yet unfamiliar surroundings to a large stone fountain shaped like a massive red scarab. Standing near it was a distinguished gentleman, his attire speaking of sophistication and wealth—a gray dress coat paired with a matching silk top hat, blood-red ascot, and a cane. He welcomed them with a genteel smile, tipping his hat. "Hullo, Ms. Thorne," he said politely, and continued, "Ladies."

Octavia returned the greeting before introducing him, "Ladies, may I present the Earl of Ironhart, Ignatius Blackwood. He's a member of the Scarabaeus Coterie."

Upon closer inspection, Blackwood's cane revealed itself as more than just an accessory. It boasted a silver knob with an embossed scarab and delicate pipes woven into its design. Its discreet buttons hinted at secret compartments, while thin vents on the shaft suggested the potential for propulsion or emitting smoke screens, making it more than a mere walking aid.

"What's the Scaraba—" Ruby lost the words.

Octavia interjected, "The Scarabaeus Coterie is an exclusive society whose members are dedicated to safeguarding antiquities from, shall we say, unscrupulous hands."

Ruby's mind faltered. Could this be the secret society Lavoie had spoken of? She wasn't sure, but after thinking about it, she dismissed the idea. If they were willing to help Asher, it seemed unlikely. Besides, members of a secret society, she imagined, were more like that hooded, cloaked figure—an ominous presence, unlike the sophisticated gentleman who stood before her.

Blackwood smirked lightly. "And who might your lovely counterparts be?"

"My name is Ruby, Ruby Blood, and this here's Mollie, Mollie Night."

"Blood, eh? Not by chance a relative of the infamous Thomas Blood of the sovereign's jewels?" he asked, not addressing her directly but curiously looking at Octavia instead. She nodded in response, and he continued, "I dare say, that is splendid! It's a pleasure to make your acquaintance, ladies."

"Ignatius, I'm sorry but we have no more time for pleasantries, a friend of theirs is suffering under the Scarlet Scarab's Curse," Octavia said with insistence.

Blackwood and Octavia led them to a shop adorned with a small striped awning. The red-lettered sign above read: Worshipful Society of Apothecaries. Upon crossing the threshold, a peculiar blend of tinctures and powders tickled their noses, enveloping them in an aromatic cloud. A spectrum of vials lined the shelves, each filled with liquids that ranged from delicate pastel hues to deep, earthy umber tones.

"Indeed. We can procure many cures here to remedy ancient curses. The Scarlet Scarab Curse is a tough one though, but we shall do our very best," Blackwood assured, radiating confidence and capability. He turned to Octavia, engaging in a hushed discussion with several alchemists who feverishly scribbled notes into leather folios before vanishing into the backroom with Blackwood and Octavia.

Waiting patiently in the main room, Ruby and Mollie observed the other bustling alchemists. The atmosphere buzzed with a sense of productivity, their movements meticulous and engrossing. They manipulated a frothy liquid within an elaborate device, which promptly churned to life, belching colorful puffs of vapors and acrid smoke into the air.

"What's that do?" Mollie asked through muffled hands. The alchemists ignored her question and continued with their work.

Ruby giggled and rolled her eyes at Mollie. "Guess they're not the friendly sort," she remarked, pinching her nose closed.

When the others reappeared, Octavia shared reassuring words. "Don't fret, ladies. I explained all about the mark of the scarab and how you unknowingly transferred it. Blackwood will bring the remedy back to the museum and administer it himself."

"Did he say how, is it a potion, a charm, an elixir?" Ruby inquired, her voice trembling.

Octavia stepped closer, her tone somber yet encouraging. "Anything that can disrupt this connection is paramount," she said, scanning the room and added, "I have every confidence in these gentlemen. We are in very good hands."

Blackwood emerged from the backroom, wiping his hands clean with a white cloth. "Now, now. We've delved into similar cases before. It's a matter of concoction, precision, and a touch of the arcane," he assured, meeting Ruby's eyes with a comforting gaze. "Leave it with us, Miss Blood. We shall brew a dram that will alleviate your friend's burden. I promise."

Relief flooded through Ruby and Mollie as they watched the alchemists mix and draw a medicinal, rosy-colored tincture. Their movements were purposeful, and each step was executed with precision. Moments later, a bright red ampoule was produced, which was combined with a smoky black ampoule, the resulting mixture bubbling before settling into a rich, blood-red hue. It was then carefully corked, packed into a small straw-filled box, and bound by a twine bow.

They exited the apothecary and bid farewell to the clandestine realm of the Scarabaeus Coterie. The heat immediately hit them as, once again, they walked through the cherry-colored haze back into the desert.

Blackwood commandeered the sand crawler, hurtling them back to the museum at a speed that far surpassed Octavia's swiftness. As they tore across the dunes, Blackwood couldn't contain his enthusiasm. "Hold on tight, ladies! We'll have Asher right as rain in no time!"

The girls gripped the sides of the buggy tightly, their curls whipping fiercely in the wind. Ruby's loose strands of hair danced like wild flames of red, swirling around her face in a fiery frenzy. Despite the engine's deafening roar, their shared optimism permeated the air, palpable and electric, driving them forward with determination and excitement.

Back at the museum, they hastened into the room where Asher lay. He was positioned on a stone slab, shirtless, and motionless. His skin, entirely black, was striking, and the crimson streaks portentously fiercer and more pronounced. Blackwood lifted Asher's limp hand, but it neither moved nor did he open his eyes.

"Oh, God," cried Ruby. "Is... is he ..." No one replied, but then she noticed the subtle rise and fall of his chest, confirming that he was indeed alive.

Blackwood removed his driving gloves and retrieved the ampoule filled with the mystical clouded concoction. Nodding to Octavia, she wielded a curious device—a small metal injector linking it to the ampoule, emitting a gentle hiss. The needle was long and thin, like a stinger on a wasp. Tilting Asher's chin to one side, Blackwood carefully

administered the shot into his neck. The girls knelt beside him, their hearts heavy with anticipation. But with each passing moment, there was no change in Asher.
    No movement.
    No relief.

15

"I feared as much," Blackwood admitted with a solemn shake of his head.

Ruby softly caressed Asher's forehead with her gloved hand. At her touch, his eyes snapped open, but 'eyes' hardly described it. The whites of his eyes were now replaced by black, bottomless pits, save for his pupils outlined and flickering with a fiery glow that made him look like he was burning up from within.

Instinctively, Ruby recoiled, clutching her hand over her heart. In general, she refrained from attributing good or evil to things without knowing them, but that thing—no longer a person at this point—emanated an aura of pure evil.

It wasn't a person.

It was a thing.

Rising as if possessed and under the influence of some malevolent force, Asher stood, his head canted at an unnaturally frightful angle. His stained lips drew back in a taut grin and his breath hissed through his clenched teeth. Then with preternatural speed, he advanced on Ruby. She raised her hands in a protective shield as he reached out for her. If she had a crossbow, she might've shot at it, but lacking one, she relied on the feeble defense of her hands.

With one hand, Asher seized Ruby by the throat and lifted her off the ground with an unnatural strength surging through his hands, in a grip as unyielding as steel. Clutching his arms desperately, she dug her nails into his stained flesh, her kicks, and frantic attempts to pry his fingers away proved futile. She fought with every ounce of strength left in her, gasping for air as her lungs constricted under his unrelenting hold. The others rushed to intervene, trying desperately to pry his grip loose, but Asher's hold remained unyielding, impervious to their efforts.

Numbly, without warning, Asher dropped Ruby. She collapsed like a limp ragdoll onto the ground with a thud. She coughed violently as she struggled to regain her breath, her eyes fixed on Asher.

Then she saw it.

There was no mistaking it.

Clenched tightly in his closed fist was the scarlet scarab amulet.

Somehow, he had retrieved it from Lavoie's mechanical pouch, the discarded protective glass glinting on the floor.

In an enigmatic tongue, he murmured a few cryptic words, possibly ancient Egyptian, before crossing his arms with a deliberate gesture, cradling the amulet against his dark chest. A billowing cloud of black smoke whisked him away into nothingness, dissipating into a swirling vortex of nebulous smoke. Those left behind stood in a state of bewildered shock, unable to comprehend what they had just witnessed. The air was thick with evil and terror.

Ruby, shaky and unsettled, exchanged looks of confusion with the others. Questions lingered in her mind: Had the injection caused this? Where did he go? How could they possibly find him? And most pressing of all, what further powers lie hidden within the scarlet scarab amulet?

Suddenly, the dark sooty ashes left in his wake began to swirl and coalesce, forming a series of intricate hieroglyphics etched before them in dark, swirling patterns of ash. Each symbol seemed to pulse with an otherworldly energy, casting an eerie glow in the dim light of the chamber.

Octavia stepped forward and interpreted the symbols. "Unlock your destiny at the Pharoah of the Scarlet Scarab's tomb..." Her complexion drained of color as she turned to Ruby, her urgency palpable. "*Ruby.*"

Blackwood regarded Ruby as an inventor observing a prototype on the verge of its maiden operation. "It appears Asher's disappearance and mysterious message have set a new path for you, my dear," he said. "Are you ready to delve into the secrets of the past and face the dangers that lie ahead?"

Octavia's gaze shifted back to Ruby, her words lingering in the air. "That is a discovery we shall unearth within the secrets of the pharaoh's tomb."

As the sun went down that afternoon, they stood at the entrance to Pharoah Aketankhen Neferet's tomb, a sudden gust of wind whipped through the air, carrying with it a whirl of sand particles that glittered and turned in the fading light. The entrance of the tomb was flanked by a pair of towering statues of Isis and Osiris, both pale, weatherworn, holding ankh-shaped rods adorned with scarabs.

An incessant buzzing seized Ruby's attention. A dizzying look into the sun revealed a fleet of scarab drones, their metallic wings beating feverishly as they patrolled the site in mesmerizing circular patterns.

Blackwood's sightline followed Ruby's and he explained, "Regrettable, my dear, but absolutely necessary. There are many unsavory thieves about." His gaze flickered briefly between Ruby and Mollie, stirring an unfamiliar pang of guilt within them. They were being led right into a treasure trove, yet they hadn't revealed any of their clandestine abilities. It was as if they were deceiving their guide, leading him to believe they were mere amateurs in the art of thievery.

As they entered the first underground chamber, luminescent tubes, and floating solar discs, cast a gentle glow over the ancient stones, painting flickering shadows along the walls, creating an otherworldly ambiance.

Whilst venturing deeper into the tomb, the atmosphere shifted, the air turning dense and cool—a stark departure from the heat outside. Their fan-laden torches created a cool florescent light that seeped through glass tubes casting concentrated beams of light that highlighted faded murals, each narrating the tales of a long-forgotten dynasty. The scent of ancient dust lingered, weaving through the stagnant air, while the ground beneath their feet became increasingly level, hinting at the passage of centuries undisturbed.

In the heart of the chamber, Blackwood and Octavia paused to examine several artifacts—Canopic jars, clay pots, viper-like coils of burnt hemp, ancient tools, and deity statues. With reverence, they picked up each item, their eyes glowing with fascination and respect as if each object held a profound significance. Mollie trailed closely behind, observing their every move with keen interest, diligently jotting down notes in her journal.

Ruby watched all of this happen as if in a fevered dream, head throbbing, a dull buzzing in her brain. Her eyes locked on the luminous centerpiece—a silver sarcophagus adorned with intricate engravings and a colossal red scarab perched atop its lid. The scarab's crimson hue contrasted starkly against the gleaming silver, its finely etched features seeming poised for animation, hinting at potential movement.

Octavia's voice resonated from behind Ruby, measured and steady. "The scarab is the key. It holds the essence of the curse, the cornerstone of an ancient power, a force that can be both a blessing and a curse."

"A blessing?" Ruby asked in shock.

Octavia nodded gravely. "It's a binding force... the scarab's power is tethered to some archaic charm yet to be fully understood."

Blackwood advanced toward the sarcophagus, wielding a multi-lens tool—a contraption that whirred to life as he aimed it at the ancient carvings. His gaze remained fixed on the engravings as he addressed them. "This ingenious device allows us to unravel the hidden mechanisms within these artifacts," he remarked, his focus unwavering. "And naturally, discerning their secrets for a more profound understanding."

The burial chamber's pervasive scarab motifs enveloped Ruby. They seemed to whisper cryptic mysteries, long kept hidden, eager to be unearthed. Each etching, every symbol seemed to pulse with the weight of history, urging her forward in the relentless pursuit of understanding her connection to the Scarlet Scarab Pharoah and discovering a cure for Asher.

Octavia extracted something slender and metal from her valise and skillfully maneuvered it across the back wall adorned with rows upon rows of hieroglyphics.

With deft precision, the rod's tip glowed unraveling the ancient messages.

"Bloody brilliant," Mollie muttered, momentarily awestruck.

"Indeed, it is," Octavia reflected, her gaze fixed on the wand in her hands. "This is a Sacred Scribe, a decoder wand," she explained. "It interprets ancient symbols, albeit with a touch of subjective understanding."

"Subjective?" Ruby asked.

"Translations might represent something entirely different—ancient principles beyond our current understanding," Octavia elaborated. "The depth of historical context it provides could lead us down unforeseen and perilous paths."

16

Octavia continued deciphering hieroglyphics on a wall adjacent to a faded mural of a scarab. One could discern that long ago, it was a vibrant cerise, but now, it had faded into a muted pink. "The Curse of the Scarlet Scarab binds the bearer to their ancestral past, woven through the sands of time," she said. "To sever this curse, the scarlet scarab amulet and scepter must be attuned to a resonance, therefore ending the curse."

Meticulously transcribing the deciphered hieroglyphics into her journal, Mollie's hand raced across the pages, diligently capturing every detail, as if etching history itself onto paper.

Meanwhile, Ruby grappled with the haunting phrase, 'the sands of time.' The words echoed in her mind, a persistent reminder of the mysterious forces at play. She recalled hearing that very phrase from Lavoie, the Egyptian merchant in London, and now Octavia.

Since arriving in Egypt, each step forward felt like Ruby was treading upon quicksand—a perilous path that threatened, at any moment, to consume her with its uncertainties. Growing increasingly frustrated with each unanswered riddle, she blurted out, "Where *is* Asher? And *how* are we going to save him?" she took a deep breath, let it out, and continued, "I want answers. Now!"

Octavia closed her eyes, regarding Ruby's outburst passively. "We simply do not know. We must proceed carefully and persist in our search." She continued busying herself with the engravings.

The flames of anger reignited within Ruby, starting with a warmth in her ears that spread to her flushed cheeks. She still didn't have any answers. She began to wonder if she ever would. With mounting frustration, she unleashed her pent-up emotions on a nearby wall, punching it with the side of her fist.

As soon as she her hand made contact, a disembodied voice filled the chamber, with undeniable urgency, calling her name. "*Blood!*"

"Mollie, did you hear that?" Ruby asked, but Mollie just shrugged, seeming oblivious to the strange occurrence.

Blackwood, however, reacted differently. His brow furrowed casting dark shadows, and he fixed his eyes on Ruby, her fist still poised against the wall. "Do not touch the walls!" his voice boomed. "Proceed with extreme caution. They conceal much more than mere inscriptions."

Suddenly, as if the wall understood Blackwood's warning, a sound reminiscent of the morning train barreling through Bricklayers' Arms rumbled through the chamber, a foreboding tremor seizing the air. Dust and debris cascaded from the ceiling, a grim indicator of an imminent shift in the atmosphere. The chamber shook beneath their feet, unleashing currents of force that shattered a stone archway and splintered wooden support beams as if they were mere crusts of bread. The ground buckled and cracked, revealing a deep chasm shrouded in impenetrable darkness.

"What... the... hell?" Ruby's voice trembled as her heart jumped into her throat hard enough to choke her.

Mollie grabbed Ruby's arm just as her boot slipped, teetering precariously on the edge of the void. Pebbles clinked down the incline, echoing a warning.

"It's a trap!" Blackwood confirmed, urgently sharpening his tone.

Still clutching Ruby's arm, Mollie's eyes widened in panic. "What do we do? What do we do?"

"Mollie, look!" Ruby called out above the tumult, pointing toward the peculiar movement. Amidst the shifting and rumbling ground, hieroglyphs began to glow eerily, casting a spectral hue across the chamber. Those embellished with depictions of scarabs and winged deities appeared to stir and animate. But Mollie, shielding her eyes from the crumbling dust, did not see.

As the tremors intensified, wisps of white smoke began to spiral upward from the sealed sarcophagus. Gradually, these tendrils transformed into spurts of hot steam, sizzling and snapping like bacon frying. The chamber walls began to glow with the heat of friction, buzzing with supernatural energy.

"Follow me!" cried Blackwood as he began to make his way through the narrow pathway. Octavia gathered an armful of papyrus scrolls, bundled together with tweed ties and ran after him.

In the meantime, Ruby grabbed Mollie's hand. Together, they dashed, leaping over the cracked, smoldering fissure emitting blasts of burning steam and a low, ominous hum from its depths. The echoes of primordial tremors reverberated below, gradually fading like the aftershocks of an earthquake.

Outside, all around them, workers were running, pointing, and yelling. As the tremors subsided, the cool shade of Osiris shielded them from the sun. While Blackwood brushed the dust off his shoulders, attending to his own affairs.

Octavia paused, taking a moment to catch her breath. "According to the inscription, we must locate the scarlet scarab scepter and unravel the meaning behind attuning to a resonance." The scrolls she held seemed to come alive with her words, as the wind coaxed the weathered papyrus to dance gently in the air.

Frustration surged through Ruby, twisting her inquiry into an unintended shout, "What in blazes is a resonance?"

Octavia gracefully retrieved a lace-trimmed handkerchief from her pocket. Tapping her upper lip, her movements resembling a painter delicately touching up a masterpiece. "You see," she began, erudition in her voice, "In ancient times, certain artifacts, particularly the exceptional ones, were believed to possess the ability to interact with natural forces."

Blackwood interjected, delving deeper into her explanation. "By Jove, some artifacts possess an astounding ability to resonate or echo, much like the resonances that interface with various forms of energy today." The girls exchanged baffled glances. Mollie rolled her eyes and shrugged, expressing her confusion. He amended, further clarifying his point. "In other words, these artifacts served as conduits or amplifiers, each finely attuned to specific energies or vibrations inherent in our universe."

Once the dust settled, they cautiously resumed their tasks within the tomb.

Octavia and Blackwood immersed themselves in translating hieroglyphics near the entrance while Mollie worked diligently transcribing their findings.

As the moments stretched on, an irresistible allure enveloped Ruby, drawing her into the burial chamber, ever closer to the shimmering sarcophagus. The intricate engravings seemed to dance in the flickering torchlight, casting enchanting patterns across the chamber floor.

Despite the warnings echoing in her mind, Ruby found herself captivated by the enameled scarab perched atop the sarcophagus lid. The urge to reach out and trace the contours of the ancient artifact pulsed through her veins, a magnetic pull she couldn't resist. Her fingers trembled with anticipation as she inched closer, the rhythmic thud of her heartbeat echoing in her ears. The scarab seemed to pulsate with a life of its own.

With a surreptitious glance around, she removed her glove, extending a bare hand to touch the side of the sarcophagus. As her palm and fingers made contact with the cool, metallic surface, a peculiar sensation coursed through her—an electric pulse, rendering her speechless, as static charges surged through her hand, shooting igniting sensations from her fingertips up to her lips.

The air crackled with an intangible force, binding her hand tight to the sarcophagus. She struggled desperately to wrench her hand free, but it stubbornly clung, unmoving.

Help! cried Ruby's mouth, silently.

The scarab on the top of the sarcophagus began emitting a faint crimson glow, pulsating with an strange spectral light.

As the enigmatic energies intensified, Ruby's gaze fixated on a small, silver vial discreetly attached to the sarcophagus lid. Before she could ponder its significance, her attention was abruptly diverted by the sound of shuffling footsteps echoing against the chamber walls.

Her lips formed the word, *Asher*.

17

All at once, the foreboding sound of metal grinding filled the air as the lid of the sarcophagus slid open, revealing the enigmatic interior. The mummified pharaoh lay enshrined in layers of finely woven bandages, cocooned in a shroud of time-worn grandeur. Though shrouded, the countenance hinted at an air of majesty and authority, with facial features veiled beneath the folds of frayed linen. Glistening gemstones adorned the mummy's brow, remnants of a ceremonial death mask. The hands were clasped over the chest in a posture of eternal repose.

Hieroglyphs, painstakingly inscribed upon the linen wrappings, depicted sacred spells and passages from ancient texts. The bindings held a faint, lingering pinelike scent, infused with a mixture of resins and aromatic oils.

Ruby desperately tried to scream and yank her hand off the side of the sarcophagus, her heart pounding with an overwhelming intensity as the gravity of the moment pressed down upon her.

Asher's focus fixed on the scarab amulet clasped in his hand. He placed it atop the mummy's bandaged, folded hands. What was once dull and subdued with age now became bright and illuminated, its crimson glow eerily complementing the shadowy chamber. The mummy, cloaked in silence for centuries, seemed to react to the artifact's presence, an imperceptible shift in the air hinting at an awakening.

Asher turned abruptly to face Ruby, his dark eyes locking onto hers with a menacing stare that seemed to imprison her. They exuded an elemental power and an unsettling sense of being beyond control. His gaze narrowed with malicious intent, the red halos around his inky black irises seeming to burn her up from the inside out.

Unexpectedly, a ceremonial dagger whisked out of its sheath, the sharp blade glinting in the torchlight as Asher pulled his hand back. For a fleeting moment, he paused, a flicker of hesitation crossing his face.

Then, with a swift motion, the blade descended, slicing through the air with a deadly precision, slicing a gash across the top of Ruby's hand.

A silent cry escaped her lips as the blood coursed out, searing pain flooding through her frame. The crimson streamed down her wrist, flowing into the peculiar silver vial with a determined urgency. With each drop, it seemed to pulse with a beat all its own, synchronizing its rhythmic dripping with the pounding of Ruby's racing heartbeats.

As the coppery smell of blood filled her senses, she watched her blood mingle with the dusty residue, the chamber seemed to reverberate with a malicious, supernatural aura—an unseen force responding to the abrupt act of a blood sacrifice.

Then Ruby saw it.

The mummy, awakened from its centuries-long slumber, emitted a low, guttural sound from its taut throat. It stirred slightly within its ancient wrappings, its desiccated limbs twitching as if struggling to break free from its constraints. With each movement, a cloud of red dust arose, carried on a deep, otherworldly breath that seemed to permeate the chamber with a sense of dark foreboding.

Then, without any effort at all, Ruby's hand was freed. She ripped off a piece of her skirt and struggled to stop the bleeding, her eyes darting between her wound and the mummy. She watched as the mummy sat bolt upright and pointed a crooked finger at her.

"Soddening hell!" Ruby cried.

The others neither saw nor heard the ensuing chaos. But now they stood awestruck watching silently as the mummy gave a muffled moan and clamored out of its sarcophagus. Where previously it had the pitiful aspect of a corpse, now it looked almost like a man, but taller and thinner, and yet still with that covering of soiled bandages that only hinted at the horror lying beneath.

Not only was Ruby clueless about how to stop the curse—now she had to confront an animated mummy. It was becoming increasingly apparent.

She was truly cursed.

Suddenly the lid of the sarcophagus soared off, crashing loudly against the wall. As it lay fully opened, a profound, ringing sound reverberated through the chamber, marking the emergence of a crimson radiance that surged from the depths of the sarcophagus.

Blackwood's curiosity seemed unshaken, his voice carrying a hint of expectation. "Remarkable! Ruby, engage with him. See if he responds to you."

"Are you daft?" Mollie's exclamation echoed Ruby's thoughts as she rushed over to her side in a protective gesture. Her gaze shifted from Blackwood's expectant eyes to Octavia's intense stare, which bore into her.

"Yes. Do as Ignatius says!" Octavia's insistence held an edge, her eyes glinting with an intensity that unsettled both girls.

Blackwood's eyes reflected wide and mad in the dull light. His demeanor switched from curiosity to something much more insidious. "The tomb calls to you, child! Can't you feel it?"

In that sobering moment, the truth punched Ruby hard like a fist—Blackwood and Octavia hadn't lured them there for a cure. No, their intentions were far, far more sinister. Ruby winced at her own naivety, the harsh realization stabbing through her like a knife. With more freckles than sense, she couldn't believe how easily they had been deceived, drawn in by the allure of a remedy only to realize they were mere pieces of a perilous puzzle.

The mummy began to amble, its erratic movements were jerky, bones creaking as it awkwardly lurched forward, its desiccated fingers clawing at the air in a haunting display of inhuman animation. With each disjointed twitch, mummy dust floated, and the bandaged form seemed to hint at a spectral power, as though the very fabric of archaic rituals had seeped into its bones, imbuing it with an otherworldly presence.

Mollie screamed.

With a fast glance at her, Ruby discovered Mollie rooted to the spot, consumed in a stunned stupor, the bone-chilling terror, rendering her utterly helpless.

In a frantic rush, Ruby grabbed Mollie's satchel, swiftly delving into its contents in search of their compact Cryonic Spirit Immobilizer—a unique invention designed to not only halt spectral entities but also to neutralize paranormal abilities. A handy tool often used during séances. Among the assortment of tools and gadgets nestled within the satchel, her fingers brushed against a disc-shaped device, a unique creation adorned with gears and small vials filled with shimmering liquid.

This was it!

With trembling fingers, Ruby activated the device, its gears humming to life with a soft murmur. A cascade of glowing energy surged through the apparatus, crafting a protective field of white pulsating light. She aimed the arc of light carefully, projecting the mystical shield around Asher and the mummy. Placing the device on the ground, it held both at bay, as if spellbound by a supernatural force.

"Once we return with the scepter, Pharoah Aketankhen Neferet's awakening will be unstoppable!" Blackwood's urgent warning echoed through the chamber, a chilling declaration. Blackwood and Octavia bolted away, their hurried footsteps fading into the distance, drowned out by the distant revving of the sand crawler's engine.

The word 'unstoppable' wrapped around Ruby like an approaching storm. Then, like a bolt of lightning, the truth struck her. Blackwood had already secured the scepter, and the Scarabaeus Coterie's true intentions were now laid bare.

Ruby was in the eye of the storm.

They hurried after them, navigating the dusty corridors, driven by the looming threat and the urgent need to prevent the unspeakable from happening.

Again.

Outside, the air was still speckled with dust kicked up by the sand crawler as it vanished from sight, leaving Ruby and Mollie stranded within the tomb's confines. For a long moment, they stood in silence. Ruby clenched her fist so tightly that a bright drop of perspiration fell onto the sand beneath her feet. "Bollocks!" she cried, punching one hand into her open palm of the other.

"Come on," Mollie stopped. "There's no use standing about in the sun." Ruby was silent. "Hey, now." Mollie said, wiping her forehead with her sleeve. "Stop your pouting, and let's see what we can find to get us the hell out of here."

So, each taking their time, they meticulously searched the burial chamber. Despite their efforts, there was little to find. As Ruby sifted through relics and ancient artifacts, Mollie's sharp eyes spotted something.

"Look! There!" she exclaimed, pointing at its luminous tip glowing among the debris. She knelt down and sifted out Octavia's decoder wand. Immediately she began to scrutinize the hieroglyphics. "Just as I suspected... Octavia omitted some key details," she said, tracing a cluster of symbols on the wall. "It says here that resurrection of the pharaoh requires the scarab amulet and scepter to be placed within a machine, the Resonance Harmonizer," she paused, her gaze serious. "Only then can the Scarlet Scarab Pharaoh ascend the throne once more."

As the implications sank in, a new sense of urgency surged within them, knowing that every moment counted to prevent the cataclysmic consequences of the mummy's revival.

"Go on," Ruby urged.

"And here's the most important part: a curse awaits anyone who dares steal from this sacred tomb, a curse that demands repayment, repayment with, with blood." Mollie's eyes widened in disbelief, her expression one of shock and apprehension.

"My blood?" Ruby asked.

Mollie nodded solemnly.

Ruby waited for more from her, but Mollie said nothing. The revelation that Ruby's own blood was the key to reviving the mummy was a chilling realization. Some of her visions, and dreams might be helpful, clairvoyant warnings of the future. But only if she could figure out what they meant.

Her mind resounded with Lavoie's claim about 'a Brit who claimed to have been gifted the scarlet scarab amulet.' Somewhere, somehow, her great-grandfather, Thomas Blood, had stolen the scarlet scarab amulet.

She knew it.

And now, the consequences had caught up with her. A bit of rebellion rose again inside of Ruby. "So, how do we stop this?"

"I have no idea," Mollie said, shaking the wand as the glowing tip of the wand dimmed, winked, and then went dark.

18

Asher and the mummy remained suspended in time —the chamber poised as if on the brink of unleashing an imminent disaster. As the immobilizer buzzed with energy, an aura enveloped the chamber, it seemed to awaken, whispering tales of a distant past woven into the fabric of Ruby's present.

Quickly, the girls began scrutinizing the seams of the sandstone walls, their fingers tracing the intricate patterns etched into the surface. Mollie's keen eye caught a stone protruding slightly from the rest. With a determined push, she exerted all her weight against it, and the block shifted, revealing a faint gap behind it.

"A false wall!" Ruby exclaimed, her excitement palpable as she realized they had stumbled upon a hidden passage. "Mollie, you're a genius!"

With careful inspection, they discovered that the wall recessed further, splitting into two great slabs to unveil an ancient lock, its weathered surface hinting at untold secrets waiting beyond. But this was no ordinary lock—it was adorned with gears and cogs.

As Ruby and Mollie approached the hidden wall, they noticed intricate engravings surrounding the lock, indicating the presence of additional security measures. Mollie traced her fingers over the grooves, her brows furrowing in concentration.

"This isn't just any lock," Mollie murmured. "It's rigged with something... mechanical."

Alarm sparked in Ruby's eyes as she scanned the area for any signs of danger. "Let's see if we can figure out how to disarm it."

With a careful touch, Mollie examined the obscure mechanism, noting the arrangement of gears and levers hidden within the lock. "I think I've got it," she said, her voice tinged with excitement.

But as Mollie attempted to manipulate the gears, a faint clicking sound echoed through the chamber. Before they could react, the ground beneath them shifted, revealing a concealed compartment bristling with whirring gears and razor-sharp spinning blades, poised to strike.

"Trap!" Ruby shouted, grabbing Mollie's arm, pulling her away from the danger. They stumbled backward, narrowly avoiding the deadly contraption as it sprang to life.

Thinking quickly, Ruby retrieved a small toolkit from her bandolier. Among the tools, she found a thin, flexible wire with a loop at one end. With steady hands, she expertly manipulated the wire, slipping it into the mechanism and delicately dislodging the spring-loaded levers that held the trap in place. With a soft click, the mechanism disengaged, rendering the trap harmless.

As the last gear ground to a halt, Ruby and Mollie exchanged relieved glances. "Well, that was too close for comfort," Ruby remarked, wiping sweat from her brow with the back of her hand.

Mollie tipped her chin, her eyes still wide from adrenaline. "Agreed. Let's be careful."

With renewed caution, they turned their attention back to the ancient lock. It boasted modern accoutrements, hinting at a concealed chamber awaiting discovery.

Ruby assessed the lock, and her expertise in lock-picking took center stage. From her skirt's waistband, she retrieved a lockpick, a trusted companion that had assisted her in numerous scenarios. This compact tool held a special place in her collection for its unwavering reliability and precision. It was slender, with an extendable, fine-tipped arm housing an array of tools branching from its slender tip.

With precision and careful control, the lockpick could effectively infiltrate and bypass locking mechanisms. Skillfully manipulating the lock, she finally gained access to a dark chamber within.

It was completely dark.

Upon crossing the threshold, Mollie extracted a solar disc from her satchel. Round, flat, and smooth, she shook it, then flung it like she was skipping a stone. It hovered silently, emanating a light that illuminated a treasure trove of mechanical wonders—a collection of ancient tools and modern implements. Between the cutting-edge excavation tools lay a pneumatic drill adorned with a complex fluid system and a steam-powered winch system. Splendid, but not at all useful.

But among these gadgets, one unusual discovery stood out—a two-wheeled contraption... a sand cycle. Its rubber-coated wheels, finely calibrated for varying levels of sand depth, promised smooth navigation through the ever-shifting desert terrain, offering an unexpected advantage in catching up to Blackwood and Thorne.

The rush of smug pleasure Ruby felt at this discovery was quickly followed by her hopping onto the cycle, kickstarting its mechanical heart to life. The motor purred like a leopard, springing to life with a surge of steam energy. She donned her goggles and yelled to Mollie, "Let's go!"

Following suit, Mollie secured her goggles and took her place behind Ruby, holding on tight. The cycle's wheels skidded and then spun, churning up clouds of smoke and dust, propelling them out of the tomb and toward the temple as the sun dipped below the uninterrupted horizon, casting the desert in hues of fiery orange and amethyst purple.

Upon their arrival, the cover of night had already draped the landscape, casting a veil of darkness over Luxor's Temple. They dismounted from the cycle, accompanied by an eerie quiet, punctuated only by the distant sound of feet thundering down—threatening harbingers of Anubis guards rapidly closing in on them. Ruby and Mollie exchanged urgent glances, silently communicating an unspoken agreement to fight.

From her satchel, Mollie grabbed and put on a gauntlet fitted with spring-loaded gears and retractable, magnetized blades—a clever contraption she crafted for herself. She activated the gauntlet, the cord sprang forth twanging like a bass string, and the blades whistled through the air. With a determined motion, she aimed straight at the guards, to sever the mechanisms controlling their arms. But the blades merely ricocheted off, incapable of penetrating their fortified plating, retracting with a defeated hiss.

"It's no use!" Ruby cried out in frustration. When she looked up, she caught a fleeting glimpse of Blackwood, a menacing silhouette against a moonlit stone archway. As the moonlight fell across his face, it illuminated his aristocratic features, casting a chilling glint in his eye. Deceptive in many ways, he appeared every bit the gentleman, but those who knew the truth understood that he was a master of deception and manipulation, his facade hiding a darker, more sinister nature.

The guards closed in on them, emitting a feral snarl, their lips curling back to reveal sharp, golden fangs. They wasted no time, clamping heavy manacles around their wrists with a harsh metallic click.

Ruby glanced down. "Stupid git—using Darby cuffs," she mumbled under her breath, giving a knowing wink to Mollie, a rakish smirk tugging at the corner of her lips.

With firm hands, they ushered Ruby and Mollie into a dimly lit chamber where Blackwood and Octavia stood waiting, their expressions a mixture of curiosity and suspicion. The cold stone walls seemed to close in on them, amplifying the sense of confinement and uncertainty that hung heavy in the air.

Putting up an air of resistance, she took a quick backward step. "Ugh!" Ruby grunted. Only the solid wall of a guard's chest kept her from retreating further. She squared her shoulders, lifted her chin defiantly, and said, "Let us go!"

"No, my dear. Fate has brought us together once again," Blackwood greeted, his voice now carrying a recognizable malevolent undertone.

Octavia attempted to bridge the divide. "You may think that we are enemies, but I assure you that we are not. After all, we share a common goal: to usher in a new era of power, blending ancient forces with modern ones."

Ruby lost her patience. "What in blazes are you talking about?"

"Why, the resurrection of Pharaoh Aketankhen Neferet, of course," Octavia declared with a calm conviction that sent a jolt through Ruby's nerves.

Then it dawned on her, the depths of their delusion. The situation had spiraled into utter madness. "You're both blooming mad!" Ruby shouted.

With a swift nod from Blackwood, Octavia gracefully exited the chamber, only to return moments later bearing a long, silver trunk adorned with ancient hieroglyphics and glistening blood-red stones. With a reverent touch, she knelt, placing the trunk on the ground, the anticipation palpable in the air as she slowly unlocked it. As the lid creaked open, it revealed the legendary Scarlet Scarab Scepter. The golden staff, adorned with cerise scarabs, gleamed in the dim light of the chamber, its crown bearing a mesmerizing crimson ankh that seemed to pulse with an otherworldly energy.

"This," Blackwood declared, lifting the sacred relic, "symbolizes the imperishable lifeforce entrusted by the gods to Pharaoh Aketankhen Neferet. And now, with your assistance, Ruby Blood, it shall be returned to its rightful owner!"

"I will never help you!" Her insolence rang out in the chamber.

Octavia approached. Her touch was surprisingly gentle as she lifted Ruby's chin with her hand. "My dear, compliance is a matter of time... not choice." Ruby jerked her face away defiantly.

Blackwood placed the scepter back inside and clamped the trunk closed with a resounding thud. The dim light cast dark shadows on his face, a mix of eagerness and resolve. "Enough," he declared. "The time has come." The air hung thick with evil foreboding, and Ruby could feel the tension escalating as the pivotal moment approached.

They were escorted outside the museum, where an astonishing sight awaited them—a colossal hot air balloon towered against the night sky, its khaki canvas billowing softly in the evening breeze. The basket skimmed the ground below, while a steam-powered mechanism readied for lift-off as steam hissed through polished pipes, snaking across the intricacies of its large frame.

Nearby, emanating from a palm grove, Ruby heard the faintest of noises.

Click.

Then chirp.

She made several subtle, low-sounding clicks with her tongue, signaling Corvus to follow them.

It did.

The balloon's ascent was slow and graceful, the basket swaying gently beneath it. The wind whistled softly, playing with the edges of the canvas as the balloon drifted weightlessly, casting a magnificent silhouette against the moonlit clouds.

Arriving by hot air balloon proved remarkably quicker than the sand crawler or the sand cycle. When the tomb was within their sight, they began their descent. Leaning over the edge, Blackwood released the drop line that was caught by a pair of natives running along the path. Their landing was accompanied by a few abrupt jolts as the basket made contact with the ground below.

Within moments, more natives emerged, sprinting towards them to secure the balloon's network of tether lines and fasten them firmly onto ground hooks. Their swift and practiced movements ensured the balloon remained steadfast, fastened securely against the ever-increasing wind.

Ruby and Mollie, still bound by restraints, exchanged looks, their glances directed toward the tomb of the Scarlet Scarab Pharaoh.

19

As they exited the basket, the Anubis guards loomed behind the girls, their shackled arms being shoved forward, propelling them once more toward the underground chamber. Yet, this time, as Ruby crossed the threshold, a sharp, piercing pain gnawed at her neck, as if some unseen force thrust a sharp blade into her flesh. Grimacing against the pain, she stumbled, pausing momentarily.

A guard seized her by the shoulder, forcefully propelling her forward. Unable to regain her footing, Ruby tumbled and fell face-first onto the ground, eliciting a gasp from Mollie. The guard's lip curled and twitched, and it emitted a low growl between its clenched fangs. With mechanical precision, it grabbed her by the arm. After jerking Ruby to her feet, it dragged her through the corridor to the burial chamber where it thrust her to the ground in front of Blackwood and Octavia.

When Ruby pushed herself up on her hands, the guard kicked her down, her face landing once again in the dirt. Although she was in pain, she rolled away and leaped to her feet, glaring at the jackal-faced guard.

To their surprise, the Cryonic Spirit Immobilizer's pulsations still held Asher and the mummy suspended in time and space, frozen in an eerie stance.

It didn't take long for Ruby to devise a plan. It was a pitifully simple plan, but after all, this realm was her forte: scheming, deceiving, and slipping away unnoticed. Freeing herself from the restraints was the first step, and fortunately, she had already palmed a picklock for this very purpose. Thanks to her late father, one of the most enterprising lock-makers in London, she knew how to pick everyday locks on boxes, trunks, and cabinets, as well as padlocks, latches, bolts, and most notably handcuffs.

As the guards busied themselves unloading the hot air balloon, Blackwood poured oil into an alabaster bowl while Octavia continued mixing, Ruby seized the opportune moment. She exchanged a slightest of nods with Mollie, silently conveying that a plan was underway.

Now was the time.

Ruby's fingers tightened around the concealed lockpick. Her gaze shifted unwaveringly between Blackwood and the entryway, a silent game of strategic maneuvering. With deliberate caution, she adeptly manipulated the picklock between her fingers, ensuring her movements remained subtle to avoid arousing suspicion. She worked swiftly, her fingers deftly navigating the tension in the lock, manipulating the pick with practiced precision. With a soft click, the cuffs relented, the mechanism giving way, and they drooped loosely around her wrists.

With newfound freedom in her hands, she discreetly sidestepped next to Mollie's side. Working with equal finesse, she deftly unlocked Mollie from her restraints. As the final shackle clinked open, they exchanged a fleeting glance, their expressions a mix of relief and determination. Silently, they waited for the right moment, patiently biding their time for the perfect time to execute their plan.

As the guards reentered, Blackwood's heavy boot descended, shattering the spirit immobilizer into shards with a resounding crunch. Asher snapped out of his stance, lowering his head, his nebulous eyes fixed upon Ruby. The mummy's stillness was disrupted by an abrupt tremor that coursed through its dusty remains.

As the echoes faded, Octavia approached, bearing the trunk that safeguarded the sacred scepter. Her movements exuded a sense of empowerment as she retrieved it. She spoke cryptically, "The convergence has begun. Pharaoh Aketankhen Neferet awakens, and so does the vessel!" As she uttered these words, Bastet emerged from the shadows, its gears whirring softly as it prowled silently taking its place at Octavia's side.

Blackwood's voice cut through the tension, "Bring in the Resonance Harmonizer!" he commanded. Then, shifting his attention to Ruby, he continued, "Centuries ago, Thomas Blood absconded with this very amulet,"

Blackwood stated with a sly grin, raising the amulet triumphantly in his hand as though it were a prized trophy. "His blood is your blood, his past is your past... you are the key," he declared, his words carrying a weighty significance that sent shivers down Ruby's spine. "Did you think it was by mere chance that you found your way to Lavoie's?" Blackwood chuckled darkly.

Ruby cast a swift glance at Mollie, seeking any sign of confirmation, but Mollie's expression mirrored her own shock and disbelief. Ruby's mind stumbled briefly. Could Mollie have been involved in their diabolical scheme? No, she immediately dismissed the ludicrous thought.

Octavia's voice resounded, a blend of smug satisfaction tinged with unmistakable delight. "No, it was part of a calculated lure. You were merely a blundering insect caught in our web. Your age, that amulet, and yes, your very blood—all crucial elements, triggering the dormant power of the curse."

"But how did you know I would take the bait?" she demanded.

Octavia's smile widened, revealing a glint of wickedness in her eyes. "Ah, my dear, we knew you'd be drawn to the new French jewelry store opening—a perfect opportunity to exploit your curiosity and lure you into our web."

"Yes!" Blackwood's hands clasped together, fingers intertwining with an almost feverish excitement. "It is the convergence, the alignment of those components, that will help us resurrect Pharaoh Aketankhen Neferet." He licked his lips and gave Ruby a sinister grin. "We needed you, the amulet, and the scepter together in this very tomb, and behold! Here we stand, the pieces falling beautifully into place!"

As Blackwood's words hung in the air, the implications sank into Ruby. The realization that she had unwittingly played right into their hands, manipulated into becoming a pawn in this sinister game, sent a surge of frustration and urgency through her.

"You won't get away with—" she faltered as a hooded figure emerged from the shadows, draped in a dark cloak. The mysterious presence silenced Ruby, bringing her to an abrupt halt. Stepping forward with calculated intent, the figure cast off the hood, exuding undeniable confidence and an ominous air. "Lavoie," Ruby uttered, her voice a tight whisper.

He inclined his head in a condescending bow. "Mademoiselle Blood."

A wave of heat rushed through Ruby, like a raging volcano. "Let us go!" she demanded.

"You've meddled in matters far beyond your understanding," Lavoie's voice echoed, an air of veiled amusement tangible in his tone. "You see, chéri, we had all the pieces to the puzzle, except your blood... and now, well, you see, we have that too."

"So, you led us on this wild goose chase for nothing!" she cried.

"Nothing? Oh, quite the contrary. A splendid diversion, I must say," Lavoie said.

"But the real entertainment begins now, my dear." Blackwood's demeanor exuded the poised showmanship of a magician about to unveil his grand act. "The Resonance Harmonizer awaits, and you and your companion shall bear witness to the resurrection of Pharaoh Aketankhen Neferet!"

As if the mummy recognized his spoken name, he let out a thunderous howl. The echoes of its cry reverberated through the chamber. Asher's dark eyes remained fixed on Ruby as she stepped back, positioning herself against a wall, careful to remain inconspicuous as her captors.

Careful not to drop her loosened cuffs, Ruby slipped her fingers into a concealed pocket in the waistband of her skirt, feeling for the Esoteric Nullifier—the crucial linchpin of her plan, a compact but potent device, comprised of copper conduits and crystalline solids that promised to interrupt mechanical frequencies. She only hoped it would prove effective against the Resonance Harmonizer.

With practiced precision, she liberated the device, deftly concealing it within the palm of her hand.

Maintaining her stance like a soldier, arms behind her back, she skillfully hid the disruptor, all the while appearing bound, ready to execute her next move.

As the chamber buzzed with anticipation, the guards wheeled in the imposing machine, their joints releasing intermittent puffs of steam, a testament to their exertion.

"Behold, the Resonance Harmonizer! This machine will merge your life blood, the amulet's aura, and the scepter's power, channeling its fused energy to restore the pharaoh's reign!"

Within the Resonance Harmonizer, a complex contraption of polished brass adorned with pulsating crystals as the machinery hummed with an arcane red glow. Its gears whirled, and mystical glyphs danced, presenting an unspoken challenge to any who dared approach. Nestled amidst its elaborate framework were the scarab amulet, the silver vial containing Ruby's blood, and the pharaoh's scepter, each emitting its pulsating aura in sync with the machine's rhythmic vibrations.

Before Ruby could react, the mummy howled again impatiently and the chamber trembled once more, a subtle quake sending a cascade of dust and debris swirling around them, hinting at an impending cataclysm.

There was no going back now.

Ruby braced herself, her resolve unwavering. She made a short series of subtle clicks with her tongue. Mollie bit her lip, anticipating the plan that would be unfolding soon. She scanned Asher, the mummy, Octavia, Blackwood, and Lavoie, an unspoken challenge in her eyes, ready to confront whatever secret machinations they sought to unleash. The clash of wills and powers seemed inevitable, and amidst the trembling chamber, the stage was set for a confrontation that would test the limits of her ingenuity and courage. The air buzzed with tension as she steeled herself for the impending showdown.

Ruby dropped the cuffs.

She turned towards the Resonance Harmonizer, brandishing the Esoteric Nullifier—a disruptor designed to oscillate energies. Then she pressed the button and activated it, and a soft hum emanated from the compact device. The chamber held its breath, the suspense tangible as the disruptor's subtle hum vibrated in the air.

The Resonance Harmonizer responded with a sudden surge of energy, the crystals of varying sizes glowing more intensely as if sensing the threat.

"Get her, you fools!" Blackwood's command sliced through the air.

Before the guards could close the gap, Mollie shed her restraints, pulling back the sleeve of her dress to reveal a watch strapped to her wrist—or so it seemed. A small, almost imperceptible glow emitted from the device. Twisting the dial and pushing the beveled crown, the Temporal Interference Emitter, a modified watch equipped with a minuscule apparatus and a glowing crystal node, began to generate flashes of pulsating waves of destabilizing stasis energy. These momentary glitches in the guards' inner mechanisms bought precious time for Ruby to continue her efforts.

Ruby sprang into action, aiming the disruptor with pinpoint precision toward the crucial energy cluster, determined to disable the harmonizer's core mechanism. Yet, frustration cast a shadow over her resolve as the disruptor abruptly jammed. "Come on, come on, come on," she muttered, coaxing the device to cooperate. But despite her tenacity, stubbornly resisted her pleas, leaving her in a race against time.

20

Suddenly, a faint rumble resounded through the chamber, originating from the discarded lid of the sarcophagus. A low, metallic groan accompanied the movement. The colossal scarab, previously motionless atop the lid, stirred. Its once-static form burst to life; gears whirred as the beetle's antennae and exoskeleton unfurled like a great fan—a sentinel awakened to safeguard the resurrection ritual. It opened its mouth, if one could even call it that, and emitted a loud screech that shook the entire chamber. Funeral dust rained down from the ceiling like ash as the beast scaled the wall, moving with the grace of a giant spider.

Ruby shouted over the cacophony, "Now!" Instantly Mollie shed her cuffs.

With majestic nonchalance, Corvus swooped in with calculated precision, dropping a chrono-magnetic pocket pistol into Mollie's outstretched hand. The weapon, a sleek fusion of polished brass, burnished copper, and gears housed pulsating chambers, hinting at an immense reservoir of arcane power.

Without hesitation, Mollie gripped the weapon, feeling its weight and the hum of latent energy coursing through it. With swift proficiency, she aimed the small, ladylike pistol at the colossal scarab. As she pulled the trigger, a dazzling burst of temporal energy surged forth, crackling with intense brilliance.

The pistol's focused beam of chrono-magnetic force hit the scarab with pinpoint accuracy. The monstrous beetle convulsed as the disruptive energy engulfed it, sparking and sputtering. Gears ground to a halt, valves froze mid-motion, and its immense form began to fracture and disintegrate, fading into a shower of metallic fragments.

Taking a silent cue from the mummy, Asher nodded. A low growl escaped him as he charged toward Ruby, who was frantically trying to get the disruptor to work. In a swift move, Herodotus dashed in between

Asher's legs, effectively tripping him. The unexpected diversion provided Ruby with a crucial moment to try one more attempt to fix the disruptor.

She unclipped the ornate skeleton key—the one procured from the market—and improvised, using it as a makeshift tool to pry open the disruptor and quickly reset its internal mechanisms. As she heard the soft buzzing within the device, a wave of relief washed over her.

The Resonance Harmonizer's whirring intensified, yet this time, its once-steady glow began to falter, flickering erratically as if affected by the disruptor. A surge of power streamed through the compact disruptor, creating a momentary clash of energies. A sunburst of sparks flew as the Resonance Harmonizer struggled to maintain its resonance.

Seizing the opportunity, Ruby pressed on. The disruptor emitted a final burst of disruptive energy, causing the Resonance Harmonizer to convulse. Flames did a crippled dance around the machine as the hum transformed into a dissonant cacophony. With a deafening crack, the Resonance Harmonizer's gears ground to a stop, the mystical energies slowly fading away.

"Nooo!" Blackwood cried in dismay as the nullifier finished its work, and the Resonance Harmonizer began to sputter and emit a series of discordant sparks, the hiss of electricity echoing a warning.

It ignited.

And then exploded.

Unleashing a shockwave that rumbled throughout the chamber. In its wake, dust and debris clouded the air, momentarily obscuring visibility in the chaos. The whole tomb lurched, heaving its ancient structure.

Suddenly, a massive stone slab crashed down at Ruby's feet, its impact resonating with a deafening crash. Beneath her, the open chasm roared with muffled thunder, causing the ground to tremble violently. Thick smoke billowed into the air, choking her breath as if she had been struck by a mighty blow.

Where moments before, the chamber had been flooded with light, now darkness engulfed everything. A cloud of smoke poured out from the lower part of the resonator, adding to the disorienting aftermath of the explosion. Tears welled up in her eyes, bitter and stinging, as she gasped for air, coughing violently.

The muffled echoes of the blast still reverberated in Ruby's ears as she cautiously moved through the aftermath, groping for any sign of life. She bumped into something substantial—the sarcophagus! Navigating around it, she felt her way to the back wall, where Mollie was last seen.

Descending to her hands and knees, Ruby's fingers searched across the ground, probing through the darkness. Suddenly, they closed around a familiar leather handle—Mollie's satchel. But it was trapped beneath a heap of heavy, slanted rocks, buried under the rubble of the collapsed chamber.

Moving aside several jagged stone slabs, Ruby encountered difficulty in dislodging the satchel. It seemed tightly wedged, resisting her initial attempts to free it. With a determined effort, she used her boot to kick away the largest and heaviest piece pinning the satchel down. Grunting with exertion, she gave it one last vigorous tug, and finally, it came loose, allowing her to retrieve Mollie's belongings from the debris.

She retrieved a solar disc from the satchel, shaking it in hopes of reviving its faint glow, but to no avail. Undeterred, she pulled out a pair of goggles and a gas mask, securing them firmly in place as she braced herself to navigate the uncertain aftermath, determined to press forward despite the challenges ahead.

As the air began to clear, Ruby's frantic gaze swept across the chamber, her heart pounding with a mixture of fear and hope. The mummy lay inert once more, and the two Anubis guards were strewn in pieces, their mechanical bodies broken and lifeless.

However, amidst the debris and scattered remnants of the confrontation, Ruby noticed a glaring absence—the others were conspicuously missing. Panic tightened her chest as she realized that they were nowhere to be found.

Where had they gone? And more importantly, were they safe?

A sudden commotion caught Ruby's attention. From the opposite end of the chamber, Blackwood and Octavia emerged, appearing disheveled yet unharmed. Their exchanged glances conveyed relief as they hurriedly retreated toward the exit.

"Lavoie!" Blackwood exclaimed, as he searched for any sign of their missing companion.

Cradling Bastet, Octavia's expression darkened, and she remarked, "He's gone."

Blackwood shook his head in disbelief, adding, "No, my dear. He's far too resourceful for that!" He took the lead, guiding Octavia through the crumbling chamber. They dodged falling rubble and leaped over deep cracks in the ground, their steps hurried by the chamber's aftershock tremors.

Ahead, a section of the archway crumbled, blocking their path. Without hesitation, Blackwood retrieved something from his waistcoat and unfolded it—his cane. He aimed it at the debris, swiftly activating it. A burst of pressurized steam shot from it, dislodging the rubble and creating an open pathway.

"Through here, my dear!" Blackwood's urgent shout pierced through the chaos, his voice carrying a sense of desperation as he ushered Octavia and Bastet through the narrow opening.

Another shockwave surged through the tomb, a consequence of the explosion caused by his cane. They hurried, driven by urgency, their steps quickening to escape the crumbling chamber before it swallowed them whole.

Blackwood cast a fleeting glance back, his steely gaze fixed on the chamber as the ceiling above them began to crumble and fall, showering them with debris. Then, with a deafening roar, the rubble formed an impenetrable wall that cut them off from sight—forever.

Distracted by Blackwood and Octavia's stony demise, Mollie managed to locate Ruby amidst the chaos. "Are you hurt?" she asked.

Ruby pulled off her goggles and gas mask, shaking her head to clear the disorientation caused by the lingering smoke. "No, I don't think so," she said, rubbing her forehead.

Mollie dragged Ruby into a tight hug, silently conveying their shared ordeal and the triumph of their survival amid the crumbling chamber. As the embrace lingered, Ruby felt a sense of solidarity wash over her, a reminder that they were in this together, no matter the odds.

Amidst the debris and dissipating dust, Ruby strained her eyes against the dimness, searching desperately for any sign of Asher. The chamber, once illuminated, now concealed its secrets in shadows and uneven surfaces. Sturdy stone slabs, remnants of the Resonance Harmonizer's detonation, lay scattered across the floor, posing obstacles in her quest. But nothing was going to stop her from finding him, not now.

Nothing.

With Mollie's satchel slung over her shoulder and the solar disc now emitting a feeble glow, the girls moved cautiously through the aftermath. The crunch of gravel beneath their footsteps echoed as they navigated the uneven terrain.

"Asher!" Ruby called out, her voice a whispered plea against the ominous stillness. The rubble yielded no response. Anxiety gripped her, and she felt a sense of urgency as if time itself was conspiring against her.

Her thoughts bent on him, Asher was honest and straightforward. He had an unwavering moral compass. He was deeply certain of his beliefs, which were formed from, but not directed by the written word, research, and of course, history. He was, in short, the best man she had ever known. And he did not deserve to die.

Not like this.

Ruby's panic-filled eyes darted upon a pile of debris, where a large stone slab had crashed down after the explosion. "No, no, no," she pleaded. Heart pounding, she approached the pile and began to carefully shift the stones, each movement accompanied by the flickering light from the solar disc. As she uncovered sections of the rubble, she noticed a flash of fabric—a familiar swatch of pants peeking through the debris. Hope surged within her as she focused on uncovering more, her hands working with urgency and determination.

Then a muffled sound caught her attention—an indistinct groan. Ruby's heart leaped with a mixture of hope and trepidation. "Stay with me, stay with me," she urged. Hastening her efforts, she uncovered a section of the rubble, revealing a glimpse of Asher beneath. Her hands trembled and her knuckles bled as she pushed and pulled heavy stones off him. Relief flooding her as she saw the pile of rubble begin to shift and move on its own. From within, a hand reached out and clasped hers, its grip firm and reassuring.

With a grunt of effort, Asher pushed himself into a seated position, his arms still wrapped around Ruby for support. He glanced around the chamber, taking in the scene before his eyes. To Ruby's relief, she saw the flicker of light returning to his hazel eyes, a familiar warmth that sent a spark of joy coursing through her. The once-ominous carbon stains and crimson streaks slowly dissipated from his body. Despite the stress and heat, nothing could dull the luster of his brown curls, now gently plastered against his temples.

Ruby and Mollie helped Asher to his feet. Together, they stood in the aftermath, the once tumultuous chamber now eerily still once again, the resonator reduced to a mere shell of its former power. The remnants of their struggle lay scattered, a testament to their victory over man, monster, and ultimately, machine. However, a pervading sense of foreboding lingered as if hinting that this may not be the end of their encounter with Lavoie and the Scarabaeus Coterie's machinations.

Just then, Herodotus nudged gently against Asher's leg. Instinctively, he reached down to stroke the cat's head, his touch a reassuring anchor in the chaos. Corvus squawked joyously, its head bobbing and wings fluttering in a celebratory dance, as if mirroring the collective relief washing over them all.

Overwhelmed with relief and emotion, twin trails of tears ran down Ruby's cheeks as she flung herself into Asher's arms, her heart soaring with gratitude and love for his safety.

In that poignant moment, Asher's warm lips claimed her with an intensity that drained her of all her remaining energy. "I love you," he said, his voice a tender caress, as his fingers traced the contours of her hair. "My Ruby jewel," he murmured, his breath mingling with hers before drawing her lips to his once more.

"And I love you," she whispered, her voice barely above a breath.

He smiled, his eyes reflecting the depth of his affection, and replied, "I know, love." Yet, in the briefest flash, a shadow seemed to pass over Asher's eyes, unnoticed by Ruby in her moment of bliss.

And as their lips met again, the echoes of the adventure subsided, a testament to their enduring bond and the triumph over the ancient curse that had threatened to tear them apart. In its wake remained the resonance of the sands of time and now, the promise of a new chapter—a future free from the clutches of the Curse of the Scarlet Scarab.

About the Author

Angel Favazza is a bestselling novelist and poet hailing from metro-Detroit, Michigan. A graduate of Oakland University with an MA in Teaching from Marygrove College, she brings a wealth of educational experience as an Advanced Placement Literature and Composition and Honors Writing teacher at a local public high school.

Her literary works have received extensive publication, reprinting, and international inclusion in anthologies. She explores themes ranging from YA fiction and sci-fi philosophy to environmental issues in her writing.

Residing lakeside in a suburban neighborhood with her husband and daughter in the state of Michigan, Angel invites you to explore more about her and her works on her website at angelfavazza.com or connect with her on Facebook (@angelfavazza) or Twitter/X (@angelfavazza).

www.ingramcontent.com/pod-product-compliance
Lightning Source LLC
LaVergne TN
LVHW010359070526
838199LV00065B/5860